COMMUNITY ANNOUNCEMENTS

Nostalgic Bahamian Tales
by
Pat Rahming

Patrick Rahming
P.O.Box N9926
Nassau, Bahamas

ISBN: 978-0-615-25306-0

Dedicated to
Ethel F Rolle
My Grammy
A Great Bahamian Woman

TABLE OF CONTENTS

COMMUNITY ANNOUNCEMENTS

FOREWORD

The Bahamas is often referred to as "The Country of Seven Hundred Islands". This geographic description, while spinning a romantic image, has, however, been the source of a serious problem: how to maintain a sense of community among small settlements with little or no actual opportunity for physical contact. In the current technological framework, in which the planet can realistically be referred to as a "global village", due to the development of information technology, it is difficult to appreciate how vital the early devices for electronic contact were to this developmental process.

Before the magic of television and telecommunications allowed instant contact, remote members of the Bahamian family relied upon a small number of linkage agents: the Mailboat, the Newspaper and the Community Announcements. Of the three cited, by far the most vital was the Community Announcements, a special feature of the News report which dealt with the country's inner life. Here the core of the Bahamian lifestyle was laid out daily, through public announcement of the details of the personal and social life of its members. Here, the details of births, deaths, marriages and anniversaries were celebrated. Crop schedules, mailboat sailings and the movements of local politicians and civil servants were placed on this early electronic bulletin board. Through this device, a disperse group of islands have become a nation.

This collection of stories provides glimpses into the inner life of these beautiful islands through the effort to record the impact and import if this binding agent. And now for the Community Announcements!

1

The News

"Good morning, Bahamas. With tourism figures down by seven percent, the Government has moved to increase the Budget allocation to the Development Board. This is ZNS Radio, the radio voice of the Bahamas, and this is the morning news for Thursday........"

Louise smiled to herself as her hands swept across the surface of the old wooden table. Felix was a good carpenter. When he left to go to New York twenty-seven years ago, all he left of himself for her was this one table and one eight-year-old daughter. The table had worn well, but the daughter had not. She had had her share of problems. Actually, she would complain that she had had three problems, the youngest of which, the only boy of the group, was responsible for schoolbooks left on his Grammy's precious table. Louise's husband "Fee" never returned. Some people said he had been killed many years ago, but Louise never knew for sure. She had done her best to raise Betty. But working two jobs left little time for guidance, and with most of her own family in Grand Bahama, the burden of parenthood had taught her to be tough. So when her daughter got pregnant in High School, she knew it would be her job to help her raise the new baby.

But soon after that first baby girl, Sheila, came another, Brenda, and five years later, the boy, Tommy. Louise placed the books on the ironing board in the corner and wiped the table top with the cloth in her hand. Then she opened the 'safe' door and took out two yellow canisters, one marked "SUGAR" and the other marked "FLOUR". The 'safe' was a wire-mesh-enclosed wooden cupboard, designed to keep food safe from rodents and insects. The canister marked "SUGAR" kept the soft, brown, cane sugar. The other was used for tea-bags.

" Tommy! Boy get your tail to this table. News on."

The booming voice with which she commanded this family rattled around in the kitchen-cum-dining room, bounced off the painted wood walls, up into the roof-space, off the underside of the old cedar shingles and spread like an October rainstorm out over the other rooms, none of which had a ceiling, and only one of which was still occupied.

" In a marathon session which lasted late into the night, the House of Assembly continued the debate on the Government's Budget..... "

Bain Town, like several of its neighbors, was settled by Africans almost two hundred years ago, a mile away from the sea and the business district of the City of Nassau, on the other side of the hill on top of which sat the Governor's mansion, presiding over this still-British Colony, where thousands of wood-framed houses crowded small plots of land, often five or six in the same "yard". Most of those houses, perched atop tall, limestone blocks, both for protection against the flooding which was not uncommon during the hurricane season, and for ventilation of the pine floors, would be sharing the same ceremony as Louise and her family. The narrow streets, steep, cedar-shingled roofs, bright colors and crowded texture gave the area a distinct character, even at this early hour, when most of Louise's neighbors would be having breakfast and getting the children off to school. And listening to the news.

"........recorded its fifth traffic fatality for the year, when car number three three zero one, driven by..... "

Tommy parted the curtain from the small space in which he had taken a bath in the galvanized tub. The water had been heated and poured by his grandmother long before he awoke. He was already dressed in his school pants and socks. His uniform shirt, ironed stiff as a board by his grandmother the previous Saturday, was hung on the hook next to the door. As he grabbed his shirt, his shoes and his school-bag and sauntered into the kitchen, he paused to smell the food.

"Mornin' Grammy."

"In sports, the Tigers of Orman Carter High roared back from a ten-point deficit at half time to win a squeaker....... "

"Hear that, Grammy? Thas the game I was talkin' 'bout las' night. I didn't get in the game much, but David hit this jumper jus' before the buzzer....."

The thin mist hanging in the room smelled of eggs and bologna sausage. Louise nodded her head without turning from the kerosene stove, where the pot of grits was about to boil over. Tommy threw himself onto one of the four wooden chairs, at the same time leaning over to turn up the radio volume, scooping up the books from the ironing-board and dropping them into his school-bag. While his grandmother composed his breakfast, he slipped on his shirt and shoes, listening intently to the news.

"In the Annual Family Island Regatta, it was the "Green Pigeon Plum", skippered by Amos Rolle, finishing first in the B-Class, despite the bad weather and above-average seas. This places the "Green Pigeon Plum" in good standing for the Boat of the Year honors following the up-coming Challenge Race in the waters of Montagu Bay next weekend."

Betty had swaggered into the kitchen, clutching a short, terry-cloth housecoat. As she parted the curtain between the kitchen and the room she shared with her son, she groaned, as if in pain. Her eyes betrayed a late night of drinking and dancing. Her skin, smooth and black, was still damp from her quick morning bath, but her hair was still in rollers, tied with a paisley cloth. As Louise looked over her shoulder it was obvious that she disapproved of her daughter's life-style in general, and in the way she kept herself around the house in particular. But it was also clear that she had decided that she would tolerate her wayward daughter.

"I don't know when you guh stop usin' up all the hot water in the mornin', boy. Mornin' Mama."

"You leave tha' boy alone. He gatta be in school in half hour."

"Well, he should'a get up earlier."

She swept a cup marked "WORLD'S GREATEST MOM" from the shelf, along with a half-empty jar of Nescafe coffee, threw them onto the table, and took a small can of Carnation evaporated milk from the ice box. Then she sat down opposite her son.

Louise removed her white enamel mug from the safe, along with the loaf of bread she had baked the previous night and joined the other two.

"A low pressure system off the east coast of Florida is creating a ridge of thunderstorms across the northern Bahamas......"

"Lord, bless this food, which now we take, to do our bodies good, for Jesus' sake. Amen."

"Amen"

" 'men"

As if by silent command, the three began the ceremony of eating, quietly listening to the radio, as if they were expecting some important bit of information.

"Grammy..."

"Hush, boy. Community Announcements start'n."

"Mama, you's listen..."

"I say hush, boy. You guh cause me to miss the Announcements."

The room finally fell silent, except for the drone of the radio announcer, sharing the most intimate personal details of the lives of the people of this tiny, archipelegic country.

And now, the Community Announcements.

"The Police at the Southern Police Station have in their protective custody a small girl, aged three to four years, found wandering in the vicinity of Sailfish Road at about five o'clock yesterday afternoon. She gives her name as Enid and her mother's name as Carmel Knowles. Would the parents of this child please contact the Duty Sergeant at the Station as soon as possible."

"Mr. Garnet Whyms, age 79, formerly of the Bight, Eleuthera, died at his residence on Rocky Pine Road on Tuesday. He is survived by his wife, Leila, two sons, Aaron and Percy, one daughter, Mrs. Amanda Turnquest, twelve grandchildren, and one great-grandchild. The funeral will be held at Mount Ararat AME Church on Dilly Lane on Saturday, May 14th, at 2 o'clock pm. The body will repose at Commonwealth Colonial Mortuary on Friday 13th May from noon to six, and on Saturday from nine am to noon. In lieu of flowers, friends are asked to make donations to the Diabetes Society."

"The Member of Parliament for Cat Island will visit the constituency on Monday, May 9th. He will be accompanied by Mr Fred Mingo, Party Vice-chairman and other Party dignitaries. While there the Minister will visit the Community Clinic, where he will present a plaque to 100-year-old Mrs Carmita Davis, the oldest living member of the Party. On Monday night he will conduct Branch elections."

"A baby boy, weighing six pounds, seven ounces, was born to Mr. and Mrs. Joseph Bain of Croton Street at the Hospital at eight twenty-nine last night. Mother and son are both well."

2

GEORGE

George squeezed his wiry body through the small hole, sliding forward on his stomach, pushed ahead by his favorite pair of running shoes on the corrugated metal roof. He had spotted this unsecured opening when he and his boss, Stephen the carpenter, had been called in to repair the ceiling in the washroom of this office complex. The ceiling had been damaged when a recessed light fixture was changed. It was his job to check the ceiling structure, and while crawling through the cavity he noticed the opening in the wall, probably left by an old ventilation duct. Outside, he had also noticed that it was located just above the roof of the stand-by generator, making access easy for such an expert burglar. He had watched and planned this job for a week.

Once inside the shallow ceiling space, he found the manhole and dropped softly to the floor. A minute later he was in the main office, rifling through drawers. From around his waist, he pulled his canvas bag, in which he dropped clocks, a small radio, a watch with no stem and a gold picture frame. But this list of booty was not worth the hours of planning and watching, being cut on his finger while removing the plywood from the hole, or the tongue-lashing he would get from his mother for staying out all night. He knew she would yell at him on his return, at least until he could present her with a gift, and nothing he had found in the office so far would please her.

Through the glass panel in the door to the warehouse he could just see the handbag sitting on a table, waiting to be inventoried. His mother loved handbags. So he eased through the door, down the seven steps and across the floor, already anticipating his exit.

That was when he heard the low, menacing growl, turned and saw the yellow and black sign on the wall behind him:

THESE PREMISES PATROLLED BY MAD DOG SECURITY COMPANY.

The family of George Major of Poitier Road off West Street are asked to please contact the Surgical Ward of the Hospital urgently.

3

MOST WORSHIPFUL

The music moved from a soca beat to a soft love song, and Ephraim Curry imagined the dance floor filled with people, imagined his wife, Sheila, moving gracefully from the kitchen to the pool deck, smiling as she handed each guest their paper plate, each with a portion of chicken, some potato salad and a cup of peas and rice. She would not miss him.

Portia Farrington's husband would probably not miss her, either. He was seated under the tamarind tree, beer-in-hand, arguing about sports, already quite drunk.

Inside the parked Chevy, Ephraim and Portia were lathered with sweat, their half-naked bodies twisting in the filtered moonlight. The frosted windows kept their moans inside, and the prying eyes out. Or so they thought.

Suddenly the car door was open. There, stick in hand, stood Sheila.

"You no-good bastard! I guh kill your ass tonight!"

With that she began swinging. Each blow arrived with it's corresponding invective, as the crowd quickly gathered at the source of the commotion. Ephraim and Portia struggling to get out of the car while trying to find their clothes, took the blows without a sound. Finally, they were outside, and as Portia disappeared along the dark path towards the main road, her buttocks bouncing in the moonlight,

Ephraim tried to calm his wife. That was about when Portia's husband Neville arrived.

He had been slow to discover his wife's involvement, but having finally been told that his "woman was being screwed, and everyone was watching", he was now in an understandable rage. The gun in his hand seemed huge, and everyone ran for cover as he waved it in Ephraim's direction.

"Bang!"

Ephraim's feet hardly touched the ground as he ran towards the canal. Without hesitation, he dove in and swam, listening for the next shot, to the far side, oblivious to the normally treacherous current.

As he pulled himself up out of the water onto a dark sea-wall, a chill went up his spine, for there, forty feet away, were two huge German Shepherds, staring at him menacingly. The wall was almost a hundred feet away, and it would take a good sprint to beat them there, and a world-class vault to clear it. The canal was the only other option. He decided to run for it.

As he cleared the wall in a spectacular leap, he could feel the warm breath of the snarling dogs at his bare back. Dripping wet and wearing only his underpants, he rolled onto the verge just as an old truck turned onto the side-street. He was surprised to be offered a ride.

The driver was an elderly man, perhaps in his seventies who drove at five miles per hour and talked constantly to an invisible wife. As they drove along, the man and his wife seemed to be arguing about a son who never came home from the war. George kept quiet all the way to his neighborhood, hoping he would not be called upon to enter the conversation.

"Where you say you goin', boy?"

"Sugar Apple Drive, near the grave-yard."

"This close as I wan' get to tha' grave-yard, Sperrit nearly carry me in '46 from tha' yard. You 'member that, Ida-Mae?"

If Ida-Mae answered, George never knew, because the truck had stopped and he had quickly gotten out. It appeared she did, however, raise the subject of the son again, because he could hear the argument resumed as the truck disappeared down the road, leaving him cold and almost naked, a block away from his house.

As he slipped from yard to yard, over fences and between houses, dogs barking all the way, he could hear radios and televisions, a loud domestic squabble, a telephone ringing, and finally, Pepper, his wife's noisy little potcake hound. If he could only find his spare key in the garage, he could let himself in, get some clothes, and be gone before Sheila got home.

The back door to the garage was open, and he let himself in. He had hidden a spare key in a cupboard at the back of the garage in case of emergency. Perhaps he should have turned on the light before reaching into the cupboard, before groping for the cupboard's light switch. Better still, he should have kept his promise to repair the bare wire hanging from the switch-box. In any case, his damp fingers were suddenly stuck to the metal switch-box, house-hold voltage flowing through his bare body. By the time he fell away, he was barely alive, trembling and foaming at the mouth, crawling painfully towards the open garage door.

Sheila turned the Chevy into the driveway, still sobbing aloud. The large, wooden doors were open and she wiped her eyes as she drove in. She felt the car roll over something on the garage floor.

The Coroner listed the cause of death as accidental.

The members of Ada Chapter of Light of the World Lodge are asked to assemble at Ascension Baptist Church on Baily Street at 3 pm on Sunday to attend the funeral of Most Worshipful Grand Master Ephraim Curry. Full regalia is to be worn.

4

THE INAGUA TOURIST AUDUBON SOCIETY

The Bahamas Chapter of the Audubon Society will hold a fly-out to Inagua on Saturday morning, assisted by members of the Flying Club. All members and friends are invited.

The Long-haired Red-nosed Shuffler waddled across the airfield, his sandaled feet never far apart, as if a long stride would cause the accidental dropping of an egg. As a species of tourist he was quite common, with his arsenal of cameras, binoculars and under-arm books. Each winter, traditionally, they would flock from the cold north to these Lands of the Shallow Seas, part of numerous flocks of strangely-clad sun-seekers, each with his or her own peculiar markings.

The Bare-Breasted Strutting Queen, for example, would spend her time strutting or stretched in the sun, finding ways to burn the proof of her visit into every secret corner of her nearly-perfect body. She would enjoy the clucking stares of local roosters as much as the disapproval of the self-righteous White-Haired Biddies.

White-Haired Biddies, sometimes called Old Girls, disapprove and regret leaving their cozy northern nests, with familiar food, conveniences and automatic first-class status. Their over-sized bag of survival gear makes their flight to the sun seem like a safari into unknown territory, with deadly tourist-eating natives hidden behind every uncharted coconut tree. White-Haired Biddies flock together, careful to avoid the other birds.

And this flock included them all. Even a few Bald-Headed Whistlers, that black, well-groomed type, often from Chicago or Detroit, where the winter wind makes life barely possible. This happy-go-lucky fellow, whose colorful clothes, loud speech and passion for sports makes him stand out, was rare this far south, where there are too few familiar places to eat the same sandwich. But in this Saturday morning flock, their bright, colorful presence was not to be denied.

Of course, no flock of Audubon tourists would be complete without a Commander Bird. Bedecked in the soft grey of the pigeon, this one was as old and wise as an owl, but moved among the flock like an excited peacock, correcting everybody and everything, whistle and booklet in hand. She marshaled them all, the Bare-Breasted Strutting Queen, the Loud-mouthed Bigot Bird, the Culture Vultures, all.

The two young friends, native bird-watchers from Matthew Town Inagua, perched on a rise just far enough away not to spook the flock, announced their sightings aloud to each other, each seeking the other's concurrence on their identification. As usual, they had completed their chores, then run through the bushes to the airfield to watch the arrival of the flight from Nassau, to share their private reference-book of tourist-birds. These were the only officers - the President and Vice-president - of the Inagua Tourist Audubon Society.

Members are reminded to bring their equipment, as there will be a joint meeting with the local branch. Commodore of the Flying Club, Mr. Henry Ferguson, will also be honored at a luncheon.

5

THE MAILBOAT

The Motor Vessel Esther will sail for George Town Exuma from the Potters Cay Dock at 6 pm on Thursday.

There were ropes everywhere. In heaps on the floor, stretched across the narrow walkway, hanging from the walls, stretched from pole to pole as handrail here, a place to hang banners there, and wrapped securely around anything that could move. This made movement along the outside of the ship difficult, even as the Motor Vessel Esther glided out of Nassau Harbour on calm waters on its weekly sojourn to Georgetown, Exuma, carrying countless boxes of canned goods, countless bags of rice, flour and sugar, crates of sodas, bundles of wood shingles, bags of cement, piles of lumber, two german shepherds in a cage, six new Raleigh bicycles, a green Ford truck and thirty-seven passengers, including Sam and Peter Symonette and their uncle Cephas Rolle. Before leaving the dock, Uncle Cephas had secured a six foot square space on the deck near the stern, grumbling as he spread the sheet on the floor that his sister had caused him to be late for the "mailboat" causing him to miss his "spot", which had been taken by "some grouchy Black Point woman" with her young baby by the time they had arrived.
" Now we guh hadde sleep out here on this open deck, an' pray it don't rain."
For the boys, however, their place on the deck was perfect. It gave them a perfect view of the city as they left the harbour, leaning over the steel rail. They were fascinated by the pretty buildings getting smaller, the cars, their lights beginning to come on, moving like insects along the water's edge; the crowded marinas with their millions of toothpick masts; the changing colors of the water from blue to green to black to silver and back; the occasional splash as some sea-dweller leapt into the air then disappeared again. They would have a lot to talk about after this trip.

They had found movement over and around the ropes even more difficult as the darkness turned all of the water black, but they had circled the ship twice under the ship's lights touching every handle, looking into every port-hole, climbing the ladder to the Pilot's deck, where they saw the Captain steering the boat. His stern look as they peered into the doorway had caused both their knees to tremble.

They had also waited in a line along the narrow outside passage, leaning into the steel wall, listening to calypso music until they could get into the small dining cabin, to have their dinner of corned beef and white rice, served with a mug of weak tea. All the while the Motor Vessel Esther had bounced along on calm waters, leaving in its wake laughter, calypso music and the occasional half-eaten fruit.

Finally, the trio had retired under a clear, star-filled night sky, lulled to sleep by the almost inaudible vibration of an engine hidden somewhere below the waterline, and the slight rolling motion, the boys dreaming of their Summer vacation, with days filled with fishing trips and "rambling" through uncharted bushes, and Uncle Cephas wondering if he would recognize his childhood friends. Or if they would recognize him.

Suddenly, they were tumbling! The boys opened their eyes, grabbed onto the nearest human, and screamed. Uncle Cephas was crawling across the deck, securing his movement by anchoring each yard's progress to some fixed object or some other passenger. With one arm around a short post, he grabbed Sam by the neck, and pulled him close.

"Hold on, boy!"

Uncle Cephas always sounded as if something was wrong. His hoarse, raspy voice made him sound desperate, out of breath.

"Peter, grab my leg and come over here!"

The old folk said he lost his voice arguing with "sperrit", leaving him always seemingly out of breath. He could, however, laugh silently, without moving the muscles in his face, which fooled most people into thinking he was a more serious person than he was. At that moment, however, he was very, very, serious. With two petrified boys wrapped around his body, he crawled back across the deck towards the stern, to be thrown back towards his starting place as the deck pitched up and down like a bull at a rodeo. The smooth sea had become a raging sea monster, spitting salt water over the helpless creatures clinging to the prancing steel deck. The boat itself, splashing away in the black dancing waters, groaned as it shifted position, its loud cries drowning the screams of a dozen first-timers.

Somewhere at the front of the boat, or bow, a strong bass voice shouted,

"Galleo! Galleo!"

The voice came closer, and the boys struggled to see who was bold enough, or strong enough, to move around while the boat pitched in the darkness, and to hear what he was shouting. But the pitching was getting worse, and their meal was already forcing it's way back up. The Ford started to roll towards the edge, threatening to break loose and roll overboard, saved only by the boat's pitch in the other direction, giving two men nearby a chance to wedge the tires again, then return to securing boxes. Sam was crying aloud, calling for his mother. Peter watched his Yankees baseball cap disappear over the stern, as he pulled his younger brother closer. This must be a hurricane.

"Galleo!"

The mate's voice now seemed to be just above the boys. Carrying a lantern in his left hand and using the other for the occasional steadying, he moved about the wild ship as if there was no danger, checking ropes, securing boxes and shouting his curious refrain. He stepped nimbly over two of the passengers who had dragged themselves to the edge of the boat to empty the contents of their stomach in the darkness, and disappeared again.

"Galleo! Galleo!"

As he disappeared down the other side of the ship, sure-footed as a goat, the boys felt a new kind of pitch in the boat. Until now it had pitched forward and they had remained almost dry Suddenly, it was also rolling from side to side, as giant waves slammed into the steel hull. Sam cried louder. Peter curled up in Uncle Cephas' side, holding tight. They were now certain the boat would sink, and they would be lost in the darkness. Uncle Cephas, sensing the onset of real fear, tried to comfort the boys.

"Ain' nut'n ta worry 'bout. This just Galleo Cut!"

The word "cut" was hardly out his mouth when a sizeable chunk of ocean landed on the crowded deck, soaking everyone. Between the shrieks and curses, there was a curious shuffle, with no-one daring to move away from their anchor-spot.

"Wha's that, Uncle?

Between passes at drying his face, Uncle Cephas explained that to sail from Nassau to George Town in a large boat, it was safer to go out into the ocean, beyond the line of shoals and cays which protect the northern Exuma Cays. But at the narrow spot where the shallow Bahama Bank met the powerful ocean, there was almost always a rage, a powerful, angry sea which could destroy a weak boat or run an inexperienced captain aground. That spot, challenged twice a week by the Motor Vessel Esther, was called Galleo Cut.

As Uncle Cephas struggled to be heard over the shout, the moans, the creaking boat and the sobbing boys, the sea suddenly stopped moving. The ship returned to its peaceful hum, somewhere forward the music started again and the other people got up to change their bed-clothes. It was as if nothing had happened. At the other end of the boat, the mate's voice could be heard again.

"Black Point, three hours. Three hours to Black point!"

To Emma Clarke of Moss Town, Exuma, from your daughter, Shirley. Please meet the mailboat on Friday morning at Georgetown. I will be sending a box of goods for you and the children.

6

A NIGHT OUT

Grammy and Aunt Mae were listening to the news when I finished my bath. The brown dust which had attached itself to me on the baseball field had been mercilessly removed, left to drown in the coagulated well-water. I dressed quickly and removed the waxed paper protecting the food left on the dining table, and ate standing up. The seven-fifteen news was almost over.

As I passed through the living-room end of the long wooden house, at the speed of light, Grammy asked mechanically - and rhetorically - where I was going, then warned, again, that if I didn't learn to stay at home I would soon get into trouble, like the boy on West Street. (The "boy on West Street" had been involved in a fight in the Zanzibar, where he stabbed another young man, killing him. On the evening news he had just been sentenced to seven years in Fox Hill Prison). I was already on the porch, hurdling the balustrade when she threw out her final threat;

"....an' if yuh ain' in this house by ten o'clock when I lock my door, yuh might as well stay where yuh bin!"

My friend Pat was two or three years older than me, and had dropped out of school a year ago. As long as his father was in a good mood, he could come and go as he pleased, a fact which managed to creep into the conversation whenever I was worried about the time, and was trying to persuade him to hurry. As usual, he was ready, standing at his gate, dressed to kill. His tailor-made long-sleeve shirt was open to his hairy navel, neatly tucked into his bell-bottom gabardine trousers. Light-skinned, curly haired and the best dresser in the neighborhood, he could always take his pick of the girls when we were out. I, on the other hand, was too young, wore mostly clothes bought by my grandmother at sales, and too dark to be considered good-looking, so I gladly accepted conversation with whichever girl was left after his choice.

As I appeared, his older sister, seated on the porch, issued the same warning as Grammy. She was an unmarried woman of perhaps thirty, with two children, living with her parents. In fact, in their house - one of the largest on the street - there were two unmarried adult sisters, two unmarried teenage nieces, sometimes an unmarried adult brother and a varying number of their children. Pat laughed at his sister, and we left.

We had been invited to the wedding reception by a friend of the groom's brother. It was not important that neither of us knew either the groom's name or the bride's name. And while we knew the street where the reception was being held, we weren't sure which house it was, just that it was a "blue and white stone-building house with a hog-plum tree on the west side, and a black truck in front."

A block away we could hear Clyde McPhatter and the Platters through the tree-tops. Like homing pigeons, we locked onto the promise of an evening's dancing. As we turned into the short dead-end, we could see the familiar group of young men, each with a beer in hand, dancing and trading stories in the street. The chairs on the porch were filled with "older" people, all feasting on chicken, peas-and-rice and potato salad served on paper plates by laughing young women in their Church clothes. We spoke to whoever noticed us as we crossed the porch and entered the living room, where the bride and groom sat in all their splendor, eating chicken in their laps like everyone else. Beyond them, in the dining rooom, stood a mahogany table with the wedding cake. The house must have belonged to a carpenter, because the division between the living and dining room was one of the finest arches I had ever seen. It was made of mahogany with a built-in china cupboard on either side, all beautifully varnished.

As usual, Pat took the lead. His confidence always impressed me. Without hesitation he walked directly to the bride, nodding respectfully at the others in the room as he crossed. At the sofa he bent and kissed her lightly on the cheek.
"You gat y'self a good man. I know he guh be happy now". Then turning to the groom, he reached out his hand, waited until he responded, and looked directly into his eyes;

"Boy, I thought you'd never do the thing. Dis woman d'serve the best, an' I know you guh treat her right. Don't get up. Don't get up. Just do right. An' congrats, man."

As he shook the hands of the rest of the wedding party ceremoniously, the bride and groom returned to their chicken, each certain he was an old friend of the other. As his friend, all I had to do was kiss he bride, and shake everyone's hand, nodding as I went. We were half in.

But without a drink in our hand, we were still half strangers, so we headed for the bar. As we crossed the patio-dance floor, Lloyd Price was serenading a dozen couples in the semi-darkness. Around the dancing couples, ringing the space, were chairs, where groups of young ladies in their Sunday best chatted while waiting for an invitation to dance. Their male counterparts had all taken positions under the scarlet-plum tree where the bar was set up, lit by bare bulbs strung between the branches.
"Gimme two 'Stel."

Roughly translated, Pat had asked for two Amstel beers, the only beverage that brought instant membership in any group of young men. Eyeing him suspiciously, but careful not to break the festive mood, the bartender (no doubt a relative of the bride) handed him two chilled bottles, one of which he handed to me.

"Ladies and gentlemen, Mr. and Mrs. James Edgecombe will now take their first dance as husban' an' wife."
The bride and groom had emerged from the house and Roy Hamilton's "Unchained Melody" was floating through the trees. Everyone else left the floor and started to clap, including Pat. We had paid our respects and had our drink in hand. And we now knew the couple's names. Now we could join the fellas in the street, or single out two of the finely dressed girls for teenage attack on the dance-floor. Pat was also an excellent dancer, especially the slow numbers, which he always reserved for the prettiest girls.
The bride and groom left after their dance, but the party continued for another four hours. As usual, I hadn't thought much about Grammy's parting threat until we left the party, beer bottles in hand. From inside the darkened houses along the way, we could hear the end of the midnight news and "God save the Queen." The radio station was signing off for the night. I was in trouble.

Even with his bravado, Pat acknowledged his own concern by his quick pace. We laughed and talked to mask our anxiety, but as we turned into Scott Street, there were no formalities. We threw away the beer bottles, sipped our breath-freshening Tips, and parted at Pat's gate.

Ninety seconds later I knocked on the door, knowing what to expect - nothing. Aunt Mae, sleeping on the couch in the living room, dared not open the door in defiance of Grammy's threat. She slept lightly, and all day tomorrow, her day off, she would be complaining about not being able to get back to sleep. I knocked again, and felt a surge of desperation in the pit of my stomach. Grammy's window was on the western side of the house, midway along its length. The pile of lumber and the disused carpenter's workbench was also on the western side of the house, which made my climb to her bedroom window even more hazardous. As usual, the sash window was open; but the screen closed.

"Grammy.... Grammy."

Silence. A heavy sigh and the sound of a box-spring groaning under stress. I imagined Grammy turning away from the window, sucking her teeth.

"Man, Grammy, man, open the door."

"You's man. You could go back where y'come from."
"Man, Grammy, man...."

Aunt Mae, only a few feet away in the next room, sucked her teeth in disgust. I looked around at all the darkened little wooden houses, and imagined a dozen pairs of ears leaning towards the screened windows, laughing quietly at my predicament. I climbed down off the bench and went back to the porch, where I found a spot on the floor lit by the nearby street-light, and sat to think. My confederate was probably safely in bed by now, and it looked as if I might have to sleep outside on the porch. It was not fair.

"Grammy".

The conditioned response to my voice seemed to be a heavy sigh and a shift of position.

"I say go back where y' bin. My door close eleven o'clock. You's man, so you could go back where you could come an' go like yuh please."
"Man, Grammy, just this time. It ain' guh hap'n no more".

Back to the silence, to Aunt Mae's agitated mutter and to a quick return to the porch floor, this time thinking I might really have to sleep there.

"Hey, boy. What you doin' outside?"

It was No-Nose. And he was drunk. No-Nose lived in the yard next door with his wife Ida. He had lost his nose in a fight long before coming to Scott Street, but he never stopped fighting, despite his age.

"Boy, get y'ass inside."

He dropped his bicycle with a loud "clang" under the street-light and stumbled across the street, his hands raised menacingly. In my mind's eye, I began to rehearse the blows I would throw, to see me beating him mercilessly in th front-yard. I could already smell his rancid breath.

"You better leave me alone, mind."
"Come here, boy. I guh cut your ass t'night."

I had backed as far into the porch as I could, and he had started up the limestone steps when I heard the latch turn. Suddenly, Grammy, night-gown and all, was between No-Nose and me, raised broom in hand.

"You better get from here, you ol' drunkin' dog. Get from here!"

As No-Nose practically fell back down the steps, I slipped inside and hurried to my room. In no time at all I was in bed, trembling. A few seconds later my room door opened, and I closed my eyes, pretending to be asleep. I was fooling nobody.

"Dis da las' time I openin' my door dis time'a night."

The door closed. Through the wooden wall, I heard her bed moan again. Through my open window, I could hear No-Nose banging on his wooden door.

"Dammit woman, open dis door. I say open dis door!"

I knew how he felt.

Mrs. Laura Hart of Hart's, Long Island and Mr. and Mrs. Cephas Edgecombe of Kennedy Subdivision announce the wedding of their children, Laura-Mae Hart and James Edgecombe, at Mount Moriah Native Baptist Church on Crooked Street on Saturday at 3 o'clock PM. Reception will follow at the home of the bride's uncle on Lilly-of-the-Valley Corner. The couple will honeymoon in Jamaica.

2

SCOTT STREET

I stared at the bleached, wooden shell. Like an old skull thrown about a cemetery, this stained, green carcass stood naked in the field of Shepherd's Needles. This used to be home for Mr. Williams, the quiet Turks Island man whose accordion music signaled the end of every day when I was fourteen years old, and lived next door. My eyes filled as I turned towards what used to be my home. There was nothing there. The long, graceful wooden building which once sat majestically atop a forest of tall limestone blocks was gone, leaving those blocks and the stone steps which led to the porch, half hidden. Those tall weeds, with their pretty yellow and white flowers, had erased almost all evidence of my childhood.

But the 'Clubhouse' was still there. While time had ravaged my childhood kingdom, leaving only those humbled ruins, the 'Clubhouse' had survived and grown, and its dillies were now in full season. This huge dilly tree still towered over the carcass of Mr. Williams' house, its fruit tempting little boys. The wide branches were now even better for our special game of 'tree-top catchers'.

"Hey mister, you loss' eh?"

The little girl, who could have been seven or eight years old, had crossed the street from a house I knew well. Like several of the houses on Scott Street, it had been a house full of women. Elise, the older of two unmarried sisters, had lived in the U.S. for several years, and had what we all called "style". She was what the young men in the neighbourhood thought all women should be - good-looking and fun. Actually, Elise lived in a smaller wooden house on the eastern side of the garden, but she spent most of her time in the big house listening to music. Eurie was her sister, younger and plainer. She, on the other hand, was the model of matronly responsibility, tending to her invalid mother, her delinquent adolescent son, Elise's teenage daughter and working full time. I think Eurie was the nearest my Grammy had to a best friend in the neighbourhood. Jackie, Elise's teenage daughter, left to be raised by her sister Eurie when she went off to the

"States",seemed to spend her whole life talking to boys on the porch. The only male in the house was Eurie's son Dee, an unusually big boy whose father had also been quite big. Dee was too young to be "company", but because of his size, he never understood that and usually could be found hanging around the older boys. His dark skin was unusually smooth, as was this little girl's. Could this be Dee's daughter?

I assured her that I was not lost, and she returned to her game with another little girl across the street. I watched them for awhile, admiring the neatness of Eurie's garden. It and their old house had survived the ravages ot time, unlike the properties across the street.

As I sat there staring at the wide porch, feeling the caked-on blue paint with my eyes, admiring the delicate potted plants, the lump in my throat grew. I was feeling cheated. All the evidence of my life had been erased, as if by some sinister force. Yet across the street, it was as if nothing had changed. Dee's family had simply grown up and had children, all as though the natural order applied to them, but not to me. Even the whine of Teddy's saw was still there.

Teddy Lightbourne was my best friend Pat's oldest brother, who made furniture in a small shop which opened directly onto the street next door to Dee's house. Inside the shop were all sorts of wonderful and dangerous machines, with which Teddy could shape and trim and cut and glue the most complicated shapes. In one corner, tucked away under a shelf near the back door, was the lathe, with which he made beautiful, round balusters, spokes for chairs and legs for expensive mahogany tables. In another corner stood the drill with which he made holes for connecting things. In the middle of the floor, however, was the monster - the power saw. The heavy whine of the power saw was the signal that Teddy was at work, and the boys on the block could come and watch. Or, if they were lucky, they could even help.

There were two ways to help. You could hold the wood while he worked it, or you could help sand the finished product smooth, in preparation for the usual finish of varnish. On rare occasions, you could help load the truck to deliver the tables, chairs or cabinets.

Through the window, I could see him. Teddy was still there making furniture on Scott Street. Bent over the saw, he was like the old story-book character, Pinocchio's father working away, oblivious to the passage of time, oblivious to the decay with which I had wrestled for the past minutes, I was happy to see this evidence of my past unchanged, and I was not surprised to find myself smiling.

Rudy's house was also gone. Rudy was my friend, who lived near the corner with his mother Miss Olive, two sisters and a brother in a four-room wooden house. All that remained of Miss Olive's household was a few feet of the rubble boundary wall, begun by the owner of the yard, but never finished. Like many of the houses in the area, their house was on land leased from some invisible owner, someone with only a financial interest in Scott Street.

It was a Friday night. I had just come from playing 'Bruising' in the Woodcock School- yard, and was in the galvanized tub in the kitchen, taking a bath. Aunt Mae was talking to Grammy in the Front Room, and I could hear Uncle come in, breathless, obviously excited about a job he had just landed. Six months earlier he had bought an old truck from one of his friends, and built a sturdy wooden body on the steel frame, then painted a black 'FOR HIRE' sign all over it. He had just landed the job of pulling a house from Augusta Street to Scott Street.

I was dressed in a flash. After all, I was Uncle's number one helper. When we got to Augusta Street, the four-room wooden house was already in the middle of the road, waiting for the truck. In a few minutes we were hitched up and for the rest of the night we inched along the dark roadway with the delicate wooden structure, followed by a trail of smaller children. My job was watching for hazards, like overhead electric lines, low branches and roadside fruit stands. It was well after midnight when we shoved the house into the yard on huge iron pipes, and went back home, satisfied by a job well done and glad to have a new family on the block.

The next day I met Rudy, Miss Olive's oldest son, and over the next four or five years he was to win more of my marbles than anyone else on Scott Street. Whenever I thought of this street, Rudy's pitch-black face was always there. Now as I sat reading this physical journal of my childhood, I was more aware of the loss of his friendship than I had ever been, and the absence of his little wooden house seemed a cruel punctuation to my thoughts.

Thoughts of Rudy led to thoughts of the Woodcock School-yard. Through the trees, between Teddy's shop and Mr. Whylly's house on West Street, I could see the huge silk-cotton trees, which had been my classrooms, hiding places, shelters and play-rooms during those wonderful years. These majestic monsters with their huge above-ground roots formed perfect rooms at their bases, sometimes large enough to house the classes of twenty-odd which could not easily fit inside the small limestone-block school-house. The trunk and roots, like club-house walls, were carved with the romantic history of two generations of adolescents, who had found each other and found themselves between those living walls, found adventure when those walls became the walls of forts and castles, or found refuge from a super-sonic tennis ball, aimed carefully at their heads when those walls were part of the arena. The Woodcock School-yard was the 'Bruising' capital of the world.

'Bruising' was a beautiful game. It required as many people as you had, from two to forty. The rules were totally flexible, and subject to agreement between the combatants. The only essential condition was that a line (usually drawn in the loose dirt) divide the yard into two "territories", and that crossing that line was a fatal error. The object of the game was simply to "bruise" the opponents, usually with tennis balls. Although you could play with one ball, two balls were needed for a "challenge". Two or more people would meet at the dividing line, each armed, and stalk each other, each knowing that once the first shot was fired, he (or she) would be un-armed, and at the absolute mercy of the other team, who could then take aim without concern for their own safety. If you fired first, you had better inflict casualty, then retreat at top speed. Having four or six people at the line at once was an early lesson in high-powered negotiation.

The most feared act of aggression however was the Firing Squad. This was when two, three, four or more members of one team manage to capture all the ammunition, and then agree among themselves to fire at the same person, at the same time. This was especially painful when the target was caught in the open. I grinned as I remembered the first day I got caught between the almond tree and the silk cotton tree, and suddenly saw one of the other team members taking aim at me. I dove to the ground, and the ball whistled past my head. Relieved, I looked up, just in time to see......Wop! Right in the right eye. I hit the ground again, put one hand on my eye and raised the other, yelling, "Time!". But it was too late. The second ball left me sprawled in the dirt, both eyes swollen and almost toally blind. The game stopped just long enough for me to be taken across the yard and pointed in a homeward direction, a minor casualty in a friendly war.

Actually, I had been a student at Woodcock School for almost a year. After a mis-understanding at my first school - a Catholic primary school several blocks away from Scott Street - Grammy decided I should be nearer her direct supervision, and enrolled me in Woodcock School, where she could almost watch me from home. But it disturbed her that I seemed to spend more time weeding my outdoor classroom than "doing my lessons" so in less than a year she removed me and enrolled me in Miss Dorsett's School, a small private school on the Fort Hill. But during that year I got to know every nook and cranny in that yard, me and Rudy, Rod, Pat, Gran and David. Me and Bernard, Dee, Johnny and Roney. Me and Paula, Jean, Jackie, Betty and Barbara. And the other Betty.

As I peered though the trees, walking through the school-yard in my mind, I could see the ugly pink two-storey replacement for my old school building, filling up the yard-space, crowding out the almond trees, further crowding out my time. Only the yard was still there. As my eyes fell back on my own yard, I realized I had been wrong. All had not been erased. Through the tall bush I could just see the decayed wooden frame of what used to be our outhouse, fifteen feet away from Mr. Williams' outhouse, which also stood proudly, having fared much better than ours. It had been built twenty years later. On the other side of the yard was Miss Lottie's outhouse, back-to-back with Rudy's, both shells, but seemingly holding each other up, a curious kind of support in mutual deterioration. These tiny buildings, where perhaps we all learned to read, were the ultimate refuge. Who could get angry with you while you were "on the toilet"? Stocked with old newspapers (each with a comics page) and catalogues, I could stay inside for an hour, until the heat was off, and it was safe to go back inside the house. As I stared blankly towards my former hiding place, I realized I still read in the Bathroom, and I still hide when I'm in trouble. This realization startled me, as I had not previously connected my childhood habits with my adult behavior. This was a fascinating avenue of thought. Perhaps my "natural" avoidance of confrontation was more related to my 'Bruising' experiences than to my philosophical commitment to non-violence, and maybe my belief that happiness is not a function of wealth is related to the evidence of positive life experiences in this money-poor street!

Money had not been plentiful in those days, at least for anyone I knew, and was used carefully. In fact, sweat was almost as important a currency as cash. When David's brother was building his house, there was little money in the family. He used what money he had to buy the materials, and, as with most of the houses in the neighborhood, the work was done by his friends. Barber, Pat's second brother, provided truckage. Teddy and Uncle pitched and shingled the roof. Rod's older brother Freddy did the electrical work. And Brother's brother Arthur did the plumbing. The younger boys carried fill, concrete, lumber or anything else we would handle. Brother himself was a mason, and so when Uncle built his house the following year, he laid almost all the blocks.

No one knows how much the house cost. In terms of money spent, it was not much, but the house had been magnificent, and the group of friends that built it had always seemed very close. I craned my neck to see if Brother's house was still there, but the view was now blocked by a wall of tall croton trees. In my mind's eye, it would always be brand new, and I would always smell the paint when I closed my eyes.

As I sank deeper into my seat, enjoying these bitter-sweet memories, I remembered Good Friday. With the exception of the second Holbert family, everybody in Scott Street was a Sunday Go-to-Meeting Christian. Consequently, the whole street got involved in the same religious festivities, especially Christmas and Easter. But Good Friday was the day most of us looked forward to with great anticipation.

Good Friday was a day for remembering the Crucifixion, and was always started in Church. Food was avoided until after mid-day, when Christ is said to have given up the ghost. On the return home from the service, a family meal of fish was appropriate, followed by home-made hot cross buns. Then the fun began.

This was a day for grown-ups. From marbles to kites, street cricket to rounders, the grown-ups took the lead. Miss Olive, with her cotton skirt thrown between her legs, would squat down and shoot marbles with Barber and Wenzel. Jackie would keep score as Elise, Eurie, Cine and Patricia played rounders. Those of us old enough to be invited to play would be shocked to find how expert our parents and elder siblings were at marbles or bruising or cricket. By the end of the day we would all disperse, filled with the joy of Easter, some to listen to old stories on the porch, others to parties marking the beginning of the Easter weekend. I would settle on my porch with a lap full of Grammy's hot-cross buns to listen to Rod tell the stories he had learned from the monks at St. Augustine's Monastery. Of all my friends, he was the most curious, and always seemed to find a way to chat with the teachers at the Catholic high school, although he was never a student there. This was just a part of his special thirst for knowledge, which he would eagerly share whenever we retired to the porch, or in the street under the street-light. He would read just about anything, listen to short-wave radio and search out interesting people. He would tell us about far-away places, strange customs and legends from other cultures, as if he had travelled around the world, and while he was only a few years older, he always seemed to be offering the wisdom of age. On Good Friday night, that wisdom always seemed appropriate.

I glanced at the spot where Miss Lottie, Rod's mother's house used to be and found the same pretty yellow and white Shepherd's Needles glistening in the sun. Betty had broken my heart in that house. She was Rod's older sister with whom I had been left sometimes when Grammy went out and I was much younger. By the time I was fourteen she was becoming a woman. I don't think she ever knew how much agony she put me though those afternoons when we lay in her bed, her reading aloud to me from her romance novels, feeling the breeze blow through the open window of the pretty wooden house. Their house, which was only six or eight feet away from mine, had the usual traditional lay-out: a square divided into four more-or-less equal rooms two used as bedrooms, one as a living or Front room with a dining table and fourth as Kitchen and regular dining room. Across the entire front was a porch. Wooden push-out shutters protected the curtained openings. Betty would finish her house-work, find her book, turn on the radio and head for the back bedroom. She would lay across the bed, her pillows in the window-sill and read or listen to her "stories". I would lay a few feet away pretending she was my wife. Then she'd talk about "Reg". Reg was her new boyfriend. He was big. Very big. Now, as I sat wondering whether she was aware of my fantasies, I realized how peculiar it was to live in a house with no ceiling and only curtains for doors between rooms. Yet for several years Miss Lottie lived next door, in apparent happiness, with Betty, Rod and Granville. But that was years ago. That time had been replaced by a field of glistening Shepherd's Needles. And as I stared across the field of yellow flowers, presided over by the skeletal ghosts of my childhood, I remembered the little girl's question,

"Hey mister, you loss' eh?"

No, I thought, just wandering a bit.

I started my car, waved to the two little girls in Eurie's garden and drove off. For the millionth time I left Scott Street, but this time was different. This time I was taking Scott Street with me.

JUBAL'S GENERATION
A Bahamian Life Tragedy

A man sits
cross-legged on his thoughts
a single strand
in the communal circle
nourished by the
crackling electronic fire
feeds on the facts
who what where when
why
is this need so deep?
it hurts all
the way to Africa

These coral islands bleed
with the tears of young men
ground into the hot
asphault promises
for which they have
turned their backs on
the family fortune

This land bleeds
with the blood of young men
ground into the cold
concrete promises
for which their earth-bound fathers
would have given up
their lives

A man sits
on the back-porch of his life
drinks the coolness
of a south-east Bahama breeze
smells the sweetness
of the rich, black soil
thick with his blood
and sweat

Someone said
a son was born
to the wife of a man
he weighed seven pounds
two ounces
the parents have named him
Jubal
after his great
grandfather

It was on the news
just yesterday.

A FATHER FISHES THE SOIL

The tarnished silver soil
dances in the sunlight
like an August sea
choppy with swells
a land-mariner
searches the horizon
from a rocky bow
eastward towards the past
over cane-leaf blades
which whip the clouds
dance before the trade
winds blowing
soft and sweet
following the lines
which tug at the corners
of his ancient eyes

The land rises, falls
fights his hand
struggles against his need
to pull onions from its womb
to plow its ebony flesh, it
struggles to ignore
his Baptist seranade
a capella love-song
but its frozen waves hide
a soft heart
in love with the idea
of pregnancy
of bountiful harvests
so it yields again
as it has before
it honours the love they share
in its season

Their seasoned passion completes
the pattern of the stars
etched into the fabric
of the Universe
sowing, tending
caring, reaping
sowing, tending
pouring the sweaty essence
of his physical existence
into the soil
from which he takes
the pidgeon peas
for his daily peas-and-rice
the goat peppers, onions
thyme and sour orange
with which he
seasons his days
the sweet sugar cane
the dry cassava
for which
he says grace
to the God he knows well
they have worked together
in the field

THE SEED

The land-mariner's wife yields
to unfamiliar hands
as he remembers
his trip to Panama
where men ploughed the earth
to make a sea
where he learned
to make love
with the passion
of an October thunderstorm
and his stop in Haiti
where taffia made him sick
and he woke up
with a stranger, now
the taffia stings his throat
alters the shape
of his nostalgic smile
as his wife yields
to unfamiliar hands
his fingers are
unaccustomed to the
tilling of the human soil
and he must wait, listen
through thin wood walls
to the sounds of unbridled passion
his wife opens herself
to steady hands which reach
deep into the womb
searching for the seed
the fruit planted
late in her season
the keeping of a promise
made on a moonlit night
centuries ago
when two children
sat on a sand dune
watched the silver and
black sea rolling
onto the unquestioning beach
stroking the shore-line

as the male-child stroked
his female friend
a promise kept in fear

The night explodes
with the echo
a clap of thunder
first breath
in and out
a clap of thunder
welcomes a cosmic traveler
its journey to this life
forgotten in the instant
of liquid arrival

The sacred seed is raised
passed like a chalice
from hand to hand
a sacrament for age
a promise made
this seagull's feet will not
be shackled to the ground
its wings will not
be weighted down
by packaged dreams
the sky will be his friend
the trade-winds his highways
the tallest casuarinas
will sing his name
Jubal, Son of the Soil

ONCE UPON A TIME

A boy remembers
with his father's mind
perched on the sandy throne
he surveys his kingdom
the soft white sand rolls
down to the blueness
of the sea, his bright
diamond eyes
study the dancing light
drinks in the ocean

which separates him
from the memory
of the slave-ship's origin
mountains and zebras
savannas and the sound
of drums
his lips insist
upon a smile

A slave's offspring labors
at his own pace
along the shore
his memories are of fishing-lines
taut with mile-long bone-fish
of sinking knee-deep
in a mangrove swamp
in search of shad
of that one grey snapper
which everybody caught
each summer
but always got away
of sailing with the men
to Big Cay, the sun
rising over the bow
of the wind-pushed craft
sliding mysteriously across
a sea of glass as
the Universe holds its breath
of walking the Bay Road
in bright moonlight
singing loud songs of manhood
his memories are of
that ancient pair of hands
that once held his
and showed him
how to make
the letters of his name
in the sand.

LEAVING THE DANCEHALL

Three in a row
perfect targets for
a young man's
perfect sling-shot mind

three chim-chims on a pear-tree limb

Lightly-scented giggles
in their Sunday best
white tafeta, satin sash
shoes that would dance
sit cross-legged across
the dream filled room
three sweet, ripe sapodillas
waiting to be picked
their nectars run
across his new-found mind

There is a strange
mystical sound between
leaving and arriving
between the warm bosom
of a mother's embrace
or a proud father's handshake
and the empty
absence of direction
weather-vane spinning
on a street-corner wall
tentatively reaching
for the ground
groping for something
worth standing on
there is a strange
mystical sound
as the careless gravity
of childhood releases
on the loud biological alarm
set before time

A young man's feet falter
as he ventures out
across the dance floor
tomorrow he will be
a man.

EASY LIST'NIN'

The music drives
its bloody fingers deep
into the tender flesh
of youth, it tears away
the coating that protects
the spot where
a young man holds
a father's words
where he hides the code
with which to understand
the blue-green realities
of life. Power is
all there is
all there is
all there is
the music breaks
the egg of social comfort
exposes the yolk of power
rootless and without rhythm

The drums sharpen
the memory of Mali
make the uneven ground
of youth a dance-floor
in a dark alley where
poisoned smoke coils
slithers, strikes
the light implodes
destruction is a friend
softly promising flight
opening the tunnel mouth
young men fall with Icarus
faster each time
into the festering hole
where despair burns with a stench so strong

wise men walk away
from their children
curse their plastic wings
sink deeper into the pit
where dreams dissolve
where stomachs convulse
between flights

The bloody nails break
are lost in the
uncured flesh of youth
the wound festers
eats away the passion
of proud fathers
who once sang songs
of praise, secure
in their so-called power
whose inner eye
has seen the truth
they will someday
awake to a world
consumed by the nightmare
of a youth without dreams
flames of frustration
eating away at the shell
of the life they have worshipped
as the god of their substance

The music spins a web
which holds the fear
of the privileged
suspended in the wind
it smells of stale
Dom Perpignan and the
anger of the young.

HOOKED

Tiny fingers spin
a fish-hook
sparkling in the sun
scaley lips enticed
to self-sacrifice

The faint smell
of a rose promises
a petal of passion
two souls dancing
a mating ritual
brought three thousand
years and miles
across a history
of savage expression
written across the backs
of generations
of perfect beginnings
passed like a chalice
from hand to hand
which explode
in a young man's loins
which etches again
the memory of
his mother's hands

Jubal's seed draws breath.

THE SEED ROTS, THE TREE CRIES

Burning feet push against
lathered soles
against their own
private hell hissing
fire from a concrete
pavement. Energy
anchored like a coffin
to his impotence
a barren breadfruit
tree in an asphalt
garden. He is driven
ever deeper
into the diseased flesh
of this dying dream
to smell his own
failure, to breathe
his own agony
to taste the salt

of his own tears
like snakes, tracing
new lines in his face
biting his tongue
consuming the crumbs
of his father's pride.

Bright yellow mangoes
drag the tired limbs
downward towards the earth
his father spies death
through the smokey window
of his sleep
he would invite it in
to drink dill-seed tea
with him
to touch its chilly hand
and to call it friend
but his tears keep him
swimming in his
choppy soil, waiting
for the sweet sound of a soul
growing, hearing only
the scream
the fruit from his field
rotting in a cold
dark place far away
his tears expose a fear
he does not recognize
behind the screen
of his legendary strength.

The seed rots
the sap flows
from the tree
one tear at a time.

DREAMS ON A STRING

A dot in the distance
dances in the wind
held to reality
by a string, home-made
paper kite balanced
on a rag-tail carries the hopes
of generations of sons
high above Paradise
higher, higher
almost out of sight
a boy fishes the heavens
laughing with every tug
of the taut line
catches breezes
big as groupers, strong
as an ancient hog-fish
swift as the bone-fish
his father remembers
when tiny feet
dangled from a city wall
and tiny fingers wait for the magic
tautness in the string

A father swallows his tears
remembers the fruitful
earth of his childhood
the hunger he never knew
the promise to hold those tiny hands
to teach them
to feel the fish
the proper way
to dig cassava
or to stretch the bone-fish
he fingers the emptiness
in his pockets
and turns his head.

The line stretches
a concrete wall
is once again his throne.

BY RIGHT OF BIRTH

Gold coins fall
to the moss-covered floor
carelessly cast aside
excess by right
of birth, wealth
inherited with the
blood on the family
cutlass, with the kingdom
built with the sweat
of nameless fathers
who will never know
their planted seed
by children without roots
their empty tables, empty
stomachs a right
of birth, children who never knew
pride in the victories
of Toussaint or
the courageous stare
of Pompey when he faced
the promise of the French
Jubal curses the color
of his father's skin
promises his child
excess by right
of his clenched fist.

He watches as soft
legs unused to the labors
of a cane-field
mount marble steps
towards the palace doors
each careless step
confirms his place
until darkness falls
like acid rain
dissolves the wall
between rich and poor
black and white
releases the rabid pit-bull
which tears away the flesh

of their social concerns
exposes the bones
of their human want
the soft winds
kiss the wounds
which will not heal
with the ointment
of his passions
with the still-births
he must come to ignore
his seeds planted
wherever his finger
penetrates the soil
pidgeon-peas thrown
onto honey-comb rock
yield only tears
and the growing anger
an open sore
raw against the salty
winds, putrid with
fermenting dreams
which explode
with his manhood
in his hands.

A barracuda flashes
by the pier
memory of a sunbeam
suspended
chases the idea
of satisfaction
man take any one
he can, but knows
his place
by right of birth.

NOT ME, SIR

A heavy hand pushes
against his need
to stand erect
pine tree in a forest
man in the midst

of men, to call
his own name
with the strong voice
of his father's son
to deny the act

not me, sir
I wasn't even there
blood makes me
sick

Fearful eyes sweep
the floor desperately
searches for a hiding place
find only the reality
that the heavy hand
has made its bed
in every corner
of his mind

not me, sir
I wasn't even there
blood makes me sick

Open palms upturned
beg for understanding
a pepper-leaf to bring
the boil to head
without pain
closed palms answer
in a loud voice
an eye for an eye
crushes the third eye
somewhere on the dusty floor
caught searching
for a place
to be alone

The light falls
like powdered gold
onto the colony
of dust
in this silent cell

way-station in
a young man's dream
to be more than
his father was
or could be
it coats the room
with a daily reminder
of the promise
he would never keep
the man he would
never be. He is relieved
the weight has been
removed, snatched
from his back
an eye for an eye
leaves him free to
stand upright, black
picket in a human fence
light as the laughter
he uses to pretend
there is no pain
as time and gravity
pull his dreams
towards his reality
a seagull too tired
to fly, too battered
to believe there is a reason
for its flight

The seed planted far away
becomes a tree
the Universe spins
on its own axis, unswerved
by unkept promises
stained by the dye
of the deeds done

A boy becomes a man
searches the streets
finds only the absence
of the hands which taught him
to feel the fish
to dig cassava

to stretch bone-fish
the signs say those hands
have wasted away
in a way of life
which burns young
saplings for firewood
throws the seasoned wood
onto the heap
begging for the promise
of a God somewhere
who cares even
for a Son of the Soil

The cage keeps
the world of a man's
nightmares away.

EX-CON

A whipped dog
leaves the pound
tail tucked between
prematurely stiffened
hind legs, a father
wipes his tears away
begs his son's respect
his father's forgiveness
a wandering scarecrow
pleads to be mounted
in a field
far away from the prejudice
of his pointless past
safe from the vultures
screeching in sweet anticipation
who will not forgive
the mark on his face
he has paid the price
but the door
to the dance-hall
remains closed
to him

Closing doors echo

hyenas in concerto
frustration played
without pause between bars
heavy wooden minds
closed to keep
the status quo quo
blind spot legislated
Jubal sings his
angry refrain, with notes
of pure terror
illicit white nobility
passed in dark alleys
shared in secret
a closed plastic society
which has purchased
the power he craves
sweetness poured
from a golden cup
into the festering urban wounds
where he swims
always upstream
a black crab drowning
in his own desperation
scratches his name
in the mud
and gives in
to the flow

ARMED AND DANGEROUS

Fire bursts from
behind eyelids
stretched tight around
blood-red balls
desperation drives
a careless hand
into the soul
of frustration, drives
a father to forget
the child he hardly knows
to feed the angry fire
which consumes his manhood

49

to watch the thickening flames
reflected in the communal
bottle from which
he sips the assurance
of his power, to watch
his movie-theatre image
consumed as he performs
the deeds he must
to call himself
a man

A man feels
the boy in his heart
die with every bark
of the monster
in his hand
feels his life energy
ebb with the blood
he spills onto
the marble floor
which drips mercilessly
into his shared backyard
where shoeless children
wipe the ground
shoot marbles on
domestic mine-fields
ignoring the blasts
learning the truth
about their game
he who has
all the marbles
wins the game

OBITUARY

A man sits cross-legged
on his bed
watches from a spot
far away, his children
dance in the ants-nest of his deeds

His memories are
of days spent cursing
the night
loud enough to drown
the thunder in his gut
the voices in his head
echoes of his deeds
of sleeping with a dog
behind a pigeon coop
praying to be found
of the smell of vomit
stale and salty
in the belly
of a mail-boat whale
waiting to be thrown up
onto the comfort
of a place
where his father's hand
dug the ground
to bury his navel-string
of pretty weeds
covering fields
once used to fruitful summers
barren as his promises
to his infant son

The sky sings
its deep baritone solo
soothes the aches
in an old man's thoughts
as he looks
eastward towards the past
through the bars of his cage
which have failed to keep
the smell of his rotting world
outside
which have split the
south-east trade winds
into endless acrid fingers
circling his throat
squeezing out the last
gasp of his hope

His memories are
of someone else's gold
burning holes
in his desperate hand
pretty rings turned green
with the envy of friends
their numbers grew
thick as crab-grass
after an April rain
of feeling the rust
grow in his joints
and hearing his body
cry out in pain
of the pictures of comrades
on page twelve
of yesterday's news
each one survived
by sons, daughters
and a host
of other relatives

His memories are
of a boy saved
by the Holy Ghost
at the age of eight
back-sliding soldier
in an undeclared war
guilt worn like a nylon
sweater against the chill
of self-awareness
of the smell of failure
at his father's funeral
words never said
of sitting alone
at the lonely end
of the family pew

His memories are
of strange hands
which once reached deep into
his mother's womb
a father's dream was ready
to blossom and grow

but the seed
fell on rocky soil
the tree grew weak
the fruit rotted too easily

Jubal wipes the tear
from his hollow cheek
wipes the memories
from his frosted mind
reaches down
for one final cup of substance
from this mossy old well
writes his name
in the dust
on the floor
and says good-bye.

4

WITH THE JAWBONE OF AN ASS

"And he found a new jawbone of an ass, and put forth his hand, and took it, and slew a thousand men therewith".

JUDGES 15:15

Ella was furious. Her small hands pounded the table and her voice cracked as she spoke.

"Where is it, Ethan? Where the hell is it?"

Ethan Williams could not answer. He could only feel foolish. He had a reputation for being brilliant. Unfortunately, he also had a reputation for forgetfulness. As a child, his mother had often said that he would forget his head if it weren't screwed on. But as long as he was available to solve their current digital dilemma, those around him could be very understanding, very forgiving. But not Ella Thomas. She coudn't care less how smart he was, he would have to take responsibility for his actions. While he may be smart enough to single-handedly operate Zeke, the transporter's master computer, as well as the multitude of computerized hand-tools used by the trio, at this moment his only credential was that he had been dumb enough to mislay a piece of high-tech equipment in another time zone, and worse yet, he couldn't even remember which time zone he was in when he lost it.

The third member of this team was Derek Fynes. His specialty was laser technology, and if anybody should have been angry, it was him. Along with the transporter, the security system and the world's most compact laser cooker, he had designed a number of weapons, among them a pistol-like laser blaster he named the Light-100, or "Light" for short. It was the Light that was missing. So while Ella grilled the embrassed Ethan, Derek huddled alone in the corner of the lab, mumbling to himself, scrawling heiroglyphics on his lined pad. It would be his job to rig the transporter for its first remote time search, for which he would have to create a way for a laser beam to search through time for the object, the way a computer searches for a word in a text. Derek's strong point was his patience, although he found Ella's constant questions tedious. But then, that's what psychologists do.

It was in another time, another place, that another problem-solver lay, pondering his success. Samson, son of Manoah, seed of a barren womb and the strongest man in all the world, listened with satisfaction to his servants gossiping under a shade of skins nearby. He smiled as one of the Judaeans boasted..."and the Master smote them hip and thigh, with a great slaughter...."

"They" were the Philistines, into whose hands the Israelites had fallen. It was a Philistine woman that Samson married, then abandoned after she had betrayed him. Her father, thinking her free, quickly arranged her marriage to one of Samson's friends, which angered the Israelite. He burned the Philistine farmlands to the ground. In retaliation they burned both his wife and her father, which in turn prompted his visit to the Philistine military headquarters, where he whipped a number of men single-handedly. It was the stuff of which ballads were made.

"Master, a great company of men approach, led by the Elders and the High Priests of the Temple."

The dust billowing into the clear morning sky indicated that their numbers exceeded the population of a small town. Samson tightened his loin-cloth and walked out to meet the group.

"Samson, we would speak with you."

"What have the great men of Judea to say to me? Does it take an army of men to speak to one man?"

"We fear for our households which have been threatened by the Philistines camped at Lehi. They have sent messengers, saying, 'Bring us Samson that he may be dealt with according to our wishes, or we will do unto you as he has done unto us!'"

Samson's face began to burn. This cowardly threat proved again that the Philistines were an unprincipled people and deserved his wrath. His anger towards them was only dwarfed by the pity he felt for these frightened Judeans. For their sake, he would play along with this drama.

No-one could have been more shocked than the Philistines, at the appearance of Samson, their arch-rival, on the ridge across the dry valley at Lehi, flanked by nervous Judeans. He was bound with ropes and appeared helpless. As the company of foot soldiers started across the valley, the Judaeans beat a hasty retreat, back across the desert to what they now felt was the safety of their town, leaving the securely-bound Samson standing on the ridge.

"Look. They have taken the Israelite away."
The Philistine soldiers had reached the spot where Samson had stood, and found only the ropes.

"Or he has freed himself. See? There are the ropes that bound him."

The heap of broken ropes marked the spot where Samson had been standing. But one clear set of new tracks led away from those of the multitude, towards a rocky slope, a spear's throw away. The soldiers paused, knowing Samson's reputation, but they knew their orders required them to give chase.

Samson's plan was simple. He would lure the soldiers into the rocks, and using his legendary strength, terrorize them. But as he lay in wait, crouched behind a boulder, a strange object caught his eye. It was made of a kind of forged metal he had never seen, smooth as the shaft of a fine spear, but it was beautifully carved, more finely than the statues in the pagan temple. He picked it up, and found it almost weightless. Its shape was also strange, curved like the jawbone of a horse or an ass, with many recesses in its surface. For a few brief seconds Samson forgot his pursuers, as he began to poke and pull at the strange thing. Suddenly, as if by magic, a blinding beam of light shot from the end of the object, shattering a faraway boulder instantly. Startled, Samson dropped it and fell to his knees.

"O Great Jehovah, God of Israel. I am Thy servant and Thy foot-stool. If I have sinned against You that You have sent Your maker of lightning to torment me, I repent, and bow down. Give my heart the knowledge of Thy Will, that I may serve only Thee."

Before his birth, an angel had declared that Samson would be a "Nazarite from birth". He had grown up knowing that he was destined to have a special relationship with his God, who was surely the source of this terrifying thing. Once again he picked it up, trembling like he had never done before. He held it as he had before, and poked and pulled until the shaft of light came again. He found he could command the lightning with his touch.

"There he is. Get Him".

The soldiers were bearing down on him, swords drawn. Without thinking, Samson pointed the lightning-maker towards them and sent a shaft of light into the crowd. One soldier, the one nearest to him, flew back into the ranks, and fell to the ground, lifeless. A second shaft put two men down. Soon the company of soldiers lay scattered over the plain, dead or mortally wounded.

Convinced the lightning-maker had been sent by the Israelite God for him to rid his people of the Philistines, Samson appeared once again on the ridge overlooking the camp, openly challenging his adversaries, threatening them with his lightning-maker in the shape of an ass's jawbone.

The laboratory seemed a lot brighter. In his own quiet way, Derek was ecstatic.

"I think I've got it! I've made a laser image holograph of the Light-100, and positioned it in the transporter. If Ethan and Zeke can duplicate our last trip from memory, the holograph will find its duplicate somewhere, and signal Zeke. He would then lock onto the real thing and transport it back here."

Ethan's fingers had not waited for the full explanation. They were already pounding the keyboard. Moments later he confirmed that Zeke could indeed duplicate their last trip from memory, and was awaiting the signal to execute.

"Have you done this kind of thing before?"

Skepticism was Ella's trademark, but this time she was asking an appropriate question. She had been assigned to the project team to deal with crisis intervention, but the two physical scientists found her style academic and slow, and tended to ignore her. On the other hand she was wonderful when dealing with the "outside" world, or some of the hostility encountered during time-travel (like the crowd in Renaissance Italy who thought they were English spies).

"Well, not really....hey! You have a better idea?"
"Hey! It's your job to get the **!!@* thing back here. I didn't lose it!"
"It's not lost. It's just....................misplaced."

Back at Lehi, Samson's powerful frame had served him well. He had once overpowered a lion with his bare hands, defeated every man he had ever fought, and now he had beaten a thousand men in one afternoon. But he had done it without rest, food or water, and as he turned to retrace his steps across the desert, he stumbled and fell, thirsty. Now his prayer was one of unusual desperation.

"Lord, thou hast given this great deliverance into the hand of Thy servant. And now shall I die for thirst, and fall into the hands of the uncircumcised?"

As the sun dropped over the hills of Judea, its last rays touched Samson's tired body, then the lightening-stick on the ground near-by, and once again he was struck by the beauty of the God-sent object. He picked up the strange gift and once again traced his hand over the finely-carved surface, brushing away the dust of Lehi.

Exhausted, he sang softly as he tried more of the various knobs on the object's body, still curious. Suddenly, part of the shiny body slid away, revealing a flask of clear liquid.

The flask was like fine crystal, with a stopper unlike anything he had seen. As he turned it upside down, it began to seep out, and he tasted it. It was the sweetest water - cool, clear and sweet - he had ever tasted. Moreover he found that the instant it touched his tongue, his strength returned. He drank half of the flask's contents, then replaced it in its hiding place, and started his moon-light walk back to his camp-site.

It was an hour before dawn. Samson had not slept since arriving back at his camp. He sat on the hill, his body shaking with excitement, planning the liberation of his people. This wonderful lightning-stick would certainly make him invincible. How beautiful it was in the full moonlight.

But as suddenly as it had come into his life, it left. It simply vanished before his eyes. Again, he felt the unusual pang of fear, and dropped to his knees to pledge his life, once again, to the God of Israel, forever.

For whatever reason, the normally reticent Ella was bubbling over, as she poured champagne. Perhaps she was relieved that her job was once again safe. Or it could have been the rediscovery that her team was indeed a group of exceptional thinkers, her included, of course. She grinned as she placed Ethan's glass on the work-bench, next to the dusty Light-100. The time search had worked, and within minutes of dispatching the holographic imprint, the weapon materialized in the transporter.

"Somebody's been using this."

Derek had examined his invention carefully, finding spent battery banks, a half-empty nutrition flask, and dust in the trigger panel.

"Can Zeke tell us where and when it was found?"

"No. As far as it's concerned, it was a round trip for one Light-100. It automatically locked onto any Light-100 anywhere in time. The lock-on time and location wouldn't have been recorded.

"So we have no way of knowing if we screwed up history."

The room fell silent, as the trio realized, perhaps for the first time, the potential catastrophe in their recent adventure. But Derek would not allow this moment to be spoilt.

"That's foolishness. Look. Whatever happened happened. If we never read about the Light being used, it means it wasn't used for anything special."

"Either that or whoever saw it in use thought it was something else, maybe called it a miracle or something. I agree. There's nothing to worry about anymore. The Light is back."

"Except for you and your forgetfulness."

It was a week after the massacre at Lehi. Samson, son of Manoah stood proudly in the market-place. The news of his exploits had spread across the land, and the Philistines were nowhere to be seen. Survivors of the debacle swore that he had slain a thousand men with something resembling the jawbone of an ass. After much prayer, Samson had decided not to speak of the lightening-maker.

"....And he judged Israel in the days of the Philistines twenty years."   JUDGES 15:20

THE WARRIOR

With
TORK - A FABLE

There once was a warrior named Tork, whose people were held in bondage in the land of Beguin, by an evil and powerful overlord, Thunder. Tork had been raised by his uncle, after his father was killed by Thunder, when he discovered him raping Tork's mother Anth. Uncle Gortan, who was once a great warrior, had lost his left arm in a battle against Thunder's men, and had become a sheep herder. So while publicly he taught his nephew all about sheep, privately he taught him the expert use of weapons. He knew that one day Tork would lead his people against Thunder, and that by his secret training he would avenge both his brother's death and the loss of his arm. But in a dream on his 13th birthday, Tork saw a vision. It was a vision of a new land. He saw a land where peace and plenty existed for all, where there was no powerful overlord, where every man smiled as he worked the land or plied his trade. When he awoke he ran to his uncle and asked the meaning of this strange dream. His uncle sent him to Urdin, the Old Man Who Knew Everything. Urdin, blind since birth, felt Tork's face, and smiled. The dream, he said, was simply the confirmation of his charge. He was to lead his people, not against Thunder, but away from the land of Thunder to a New Land, a land promised by the Sages. His preparation by his uncle would serve him and his people as they would have to fight their way to that Promised Land. Tork left with a new sense of purpose, to train harder, and to begin to assemble his own secret army. Urdin died that night.

Five years later, while Thunder celebrated his marriage to yet another bride, Tork led his people out into the desert, and started their search for the Promised Land. The people had never seen a map or picture of the Promised Land. They had never heard of anyone who had been there. All they knew was that Tork, their Tork, knew where they were going.

On the evening of that first day, after he had chosen a camp-site and all the families had settled into their tents, he called everyone around the fire. He listened as the older men praised his strength and his wisdom and the women thanked him for leading their sons into a life worth the rigors of their training. Then he organized his people. He made those older men responsible for the sick and the wounded, and for the day-to-day necessities of the band, such as water and fire. The young men he divided into two groups; one group he placed at the edges of the encampment as the sentries, responsible for defense of the camp, as well as defense of the flanks while they travelled; the other group he chose to go out and fight the enemies he knew they would meet. Then he announced that in the morning he would tell them in which direction they would find their Promised Land.

The next morning he arose with the sun. As he walked out of his tent a tall cloud stood, like an Olympian torch, above the eastern horizon. Tork knew the Promised Land was to the east. He assembled his people and began a march that was to last twenty years.

Freddie Miller was excited. Since his early days in politics he had not seen a successful "No-Confidence" vote. It would take a major revolt by the back-bench to pull one off, and the prospect was sending jet fuel through his veins. Through the silence of the night he could hear crickets and cicadas making their syncopated nocturnal music. He could hear the distant sound of a late-night yard-party, where another kind of music would waft in whenever the wind shifted, and blew from that direction. He could hear his wife, Freda, breathing heavily as she slept, oblivious to his excitement, accustomed to his absence from her bed. He could almost hear his own heart-beat.

As he stood, staring out of the open window, he remembered his conversation with Emmet Christie, a supposed spokesman for those back-benchers.

"You wanted to see me?"

"Yes. But le's understand sup'm. This off the record. We only talkin' hypothetical. Right?"

"If you say so."

Christie had paused for a long time before continuing, while Freddie patiently sipped his club soda.

"I speak for seven …er….people, who lookin' at what options we have over the next li'l while. We ain' sayin' we guh lose the election or anything like that, but le's say supposin' we was to come to you as a group……..jus' supposin'."

Freddie had paused. And smiled. On three other occasions since becoming Leader of the Official Opposition he had been approached by Government members supposedly interested in defecting to his party, and in each case his own covert investigation had uncovered that they were only attempting to embarrass him. This, no doubt, would prove to be the same.

"My party is a free organization, here to provide an alternative to the present government. We welcome anyone who feels we offer a more viable alternative. We don't turn people away."

Christie had re-played that answer several times in his head before he thought he understood, then continued, somewhat like a child caught attempting to out-wit its parent.
"O.K. Mr. Miller. This what we had in mind. You know we ain' bin get'n along too well with this PM since the question a' this big project come up. At first we thought we would'a work it out, but ...."

"In other words, you find yourself in the embarrassing position of having to agree with me that you fellas lead'n us down the road to bankruptcy."

He had never been able to resist an opportunity to drive a political dagger home. But his grin had assured Christie that his offer was at least discussible.

An hour later the investigation began. The records of expenditure and the lists of contracts were copied, discussed and analyzed by Miller's experts, who fed him memos by the dozen, until he had drafted the resolution. Tomorrow he would table that resolution, and possibly topple the Government. Even the thought made his body warm. But Sir Christopher Sturrup had not become the absolute ruler of the most dominant political party in history by popular vote. He had earned his reputation as a warrior by out-maneuvering, out-promising and out-fighting his opponents, both within his party and on the outside. So if Freddie Miller thought his resolution would succeed without a blood bath he was ignoring Sir Christopher's history.

Tork's people loved and trusted him. They followed his dreams through the harshest deserts, across treacherous rivers. They followed him into battles with the most dangerous and fearsome enemies, and praised him as they celebrated their victories. He was their leader and they his people, and there could be no separation. Then one night a voice arose around the fire. It was Calupa, the strongest of Tork's warriors. He was tired of walking around in the wilderness, led by clouds, hilltops, and the sound of the winds. He demanded to know exactly where this Promised Land was.

"Has Tork led us away from our home to die in the wilderness? We have passed through many lands where we might have stayed. But Tork had dreams. Tork always has dreams. Well, I am tired of following Tork's dreams. I want to raise my children as civilized men, in a real kingdom."

Tork stood up and walked to the middle of the clearing, his back to the fire. He drew his sword and stared coldly at Calupa.

"Well, my friend, if you are tired of my leadership, you must lead. but to lead my people you must defeat me. You must kill me."

Calupa sat down, and held his head down. He did not wish to fight.

"I have no wish to kill my friend and leader".

"But you have challenged my authority. Either defeat me or I must destroy you. We cannot continue together. I can not rest my head at ease in a camp with my enemy."

"But Tork, I am not your enemy."

"Did you not question my direction?"

Calupa's bowed head seemed to signal his answer.

"Then you are my enemy!"

He raised his sword and moved menacingly toward Calupa, who scrambled away and disappeared into the darkness. Tork turned slowly and studied the faces around the fire, silently demanding to know whether anyone else would dare challenge his authority. No one else dared.

One morning, in the middle of the twentieth year of their search, Tork awoke and emerged from his tent with a huge grin on his face. They had been travelling through a dense forest, with luscious fruit and many small animals. The birds had sung them to sleep after they drank the clear water from the stream they had followed for the past year. Many in the band had noted the perfect conditions, only to be hushed by their friends and families.

"Tork will let us know when we have reached our Promised Land."

As he emerged this mid-summer morning the sun was shining brightly. He had had a dream in which he saw Urdin, the Old Man Who Knew Everything, sitting on the rock near his tent, smiling and eating fruit. This was the signal. They had reached the Promise Land.

The news spread among his people, and there was great joy and celebration. Music and dancing replaced the silent questions, and while the young men drank the wine their fathers had saved, the older men and women chose the places for their houses. Finally, as the sun set, Tork called his people around him again. He praised their wisdom in listening to his word, in believing in his dream. He declared himself King, and gave the land the name Eluria, which in their language meant the Land of Fruit. From among his warriors he chose a Council of Elders, whom he said would help him rule, and he promised to be fair. An old lady walked shyly across the clearing. In her hand was a new-born boy.

"Master Tork, King of this new land, ruler of all around, bless this my grand-child, that he may be worthy to walk beneath the branches of your trees, to carry your sword in the ceremonies of the Court."

Tork looked at her for a long while before he spoke. He raised his hand and blessed both the child and the old lady, whereupon someone offered a toast:

"Long live King Tork, Absolute Ruler of....... Eluria!"

For the next ten years Tork ruled without incident. With his Council of Elders, he established a Treasury and collected taxes, he created schools, hospitals and markets. He turned a section of his army into policemen, who patrolled the streets. He sent emissaries to other kingdoms to represent him, and received their official agents. And the country of Eluria became known as a fine and wealthy country.

"Well, well. If it ain't my friend Emmet Christie, who I understand went to see a certain Leader of the Opposition last Monday. How you doin' bra'?"

Christie was visibly shaken. How did Sir Christopher know about his meeting?

"Don't worry bra'. I don't mind. C'mon, le's talk."

Christie wished there was somewhere to hide in the foyer of the prestigious Flamingo Club. The Flamingo Club had been created originally as an Officers' Club for the Police Force during the Colonial days. Because most of the top level officers were British, as were the top level civil servants, it had become a haunt for expatriate - that is, white - civil servants, a place where the real solutions to the problems of running this country of former slaves were hatched, to be cleverly disguised as the brainchildren of local politicians. But when the country claimed its independence, one symbol of the change was the re-patriation of upper level policemen and civil servants, which left the Flamingo Club virtually without business. A clever young former policeman who had stumbled into a moneyed female relationship saw an opportunity to capitalize on this turn of events, bought the Club from Government at a nominal sum, and popularized it as a private club for members of Parliament and upper level - now mostly black - civil servants, very anxious to show how well they had adapted to gracious living. While Sir Christopher often had lunch there, Christie had heard he would be away, and had agreed to have lunch there with two of his cohorts to report on his conversation. The sight of his portly, three-piece-suited PM sent chills through his body, and seemed to freeze his brain.
"How's my friend Mr. Miller?"

"He ...he...Boy, we gat his head spinnin'. He ain' know what goin' on."
Christie's recovery was like a boxer who, knowing he's whipped, closes his eyes and jabs away at the air, hoping to connect.

"Oh, I don't know. He's got me wonderin' whether my back-bench is secure."

"Now Cap! You know better'n that!"

He was sweating profusely, although the ceiling fans were on and the room otherwise quite comfortable. Sir Christopher looked deep into his eyes as he held out his hand. He knew. And Christie knew he knew.

Sir Christopher's lunch was served in the Club-room, a beautifully appointed, private room off the main Dining Room overlooking the Terrace where Emmett Christie and his associates had chosen to eat, and the young back-bencher spent the whole hour of his meal under the feel of his Leader's eye. While the others spoke openly and defiantly about their dissatisfaction, he was curiously quiet, and made no report. Instead, he invited the men to his house later that evening. As they left, the PM stepped out of the Club Room and greeted each one personally.
"Gentlemen. It's good to see my back-bench together. I hope it's a good sign."

The PM grinned widely, somewhat reminiscent of the mad scientist in a Boris Karloff movie, as he shook their hands. Yes, he knew. There is a story about a king who found out that his most trusted advisor was involved in a conspiracy to de-throne him. He immediately invited him to dinner, along with all the most prominent people in the kingdom. During the meal he joked about having a fool-proof way of knowing if someone was lying.   When pressed for an explanation he drew his royal dagger.

"This," he said, "is a magic dagger.   Its blade is made of pure silver, but when placed in the fire, it remains perfectly cool, except for anyone seeking to betray me."

As the night grew longer and the king and his guests drank, the conversation turned to treachery, and the King announced that someone in the room had recently betrayed him.   He ordered everyone to form a line and placed his magic dagger into the fire.   When it appeared red-hot, he ordered the first knight to open his mouth, and he placed the blade on his tongue.   When there was no injury, the king smiled.

"You are indeed faithful.   Your wealth shall be increased five-fold."

He repeated this spectacle, moving down the line.   When he reached the conspirator, he opened his mouth, saw the blade coming near, and fainted.   He was arrested and thrown into jail and his wealth confiscated.

"Only the guilty have a dry tongue."

As he walked towards his car, Emmet Christie's tongue was bone dry.

Zed pulled the tattered booklet from his hip pocket.   Seven years ago he could not read, and the ideas he had found hidden between these old red covers belonged to other people.   His accidental meeting with the English lady had begun a powerful change in his life, a change which had left him excited, but angry. She taught him to read, taught him to make love like a gentleman, taught him to expect the best from life, then left to return to her London suburb. Life was definitely not fair.

The sun would drop into the Tongue of the Ocean in a few minutes. It was time for his reading. Each evening he would sit on the rocks at the edge of the sea for half an hour and read about the tenets of various philosophies, each one more interesting than the next, each one to be compared with his reality. His life, like that of so many of his people, had once been based upon automatic compromise. He lived where he lived because it was what he could afford, while he dreamt about living on the waterfront. He worked as an electrical lineman, while wanting to become an Engineer. He married a young girl from his church, as expected, while he was in fact in love with the Sunday-school teachers' wife. Then one day, after his new-found friend had left, he woke up and knew the compromises were over. He packed some clothes, gassed up his car, and moved to the waterfront. He had no house and no fixed address, but he was now living on the waterfront. The salt air, which renewed his spirit, had also cleared his mind concerning the way in which his island nation was being run, and he had begun agitating for change, first by crude letters to the local newspaper editor, many of which were never published, then by one-man demonstrations in public places. His most recent form of protest, however, was the disabling of the power system island-wide, to protest the wasteful expenditure of public funds, protest which gave him more satisfaction than he expected. While the sabotage was obvious, his identity had remained secret, and he was convinced it was his duty to continue the subversion. In the public interest, of course.

As the sun touched the fine, silver line of the horizon, Zed closed his eyes and assumed a meditation position. When he opened his eyes, it was dark, it was time to go to work.

First he would drive to the shed in which his tools were stored. Then he would collect the dynamite from its hiding place near the construction site from which it has been "borrowed". His target was a building which housed an arsenal belonging to a local gang, which the Police knew about, but which was reportedly empty every time it was raided, despite eye-witness reports of the deliveries of whole shipments of weapons. Fifteen hours ago Zed had seen why. Although the building was twenty years old, someone had recently built a false floor and a basement, leaving the main house looking as if it had been abandoned ten years earlier and never re-visited. The new basement, however, could be entered from both inside and outside. Tomorrow the cache would be history.

The headline read 'EXPLOSION DESTROYS ABANDONED HOUSE'. Zed read the story twice, annoyed that there was no mention of the fire-arms destroyed. Surely the Police had found the evidence. He folded his newspaper and drove to an isolated public telephone.

"Hello? Let me speak to Inspector Wells. Huh? No. Only Wells. I want to speak to Wells. Yes, I'll Hold.... Hello? Inspector Wells? How come y'all ain' say nut'n bout the guns what blow up in the fire last night? Don't worry how I know. I know. If y'all don't stop tryin' tuh fool the public, I guh haveta deal with y'all too."

He hung up.

Inspector Wells scribbled a note, handed it to the young female officer nearby and walked towards the Commander's office.

"Well. Now we know for sure. That was no accident last night. We have a Robin Hood out there."

"Damn!"

***

"How you fellahs feel 'bout takin' over the Government?"

As he watched their reactions in mischievous amusement Freddie wondered how many of them thought he meant by force. Ever since their island nation's Independence, there had been sly suggestions by the press, both local and foreign, that the only way to remove Sir Christopher was by force, a view Freddie had worked hard to deny, but which persisted none-the-less. But while he might enjoy toying with their emotions, time was short, so he drove straight to the point.

"I propose we move a vote of "No Confidence" in the government. We can prove Sir Christopher has ignored his own party in his blatant mis-management of the Treasury, tryin' to get this project built as a monument to himself, and I think we have the votes of his back-bench."

Silence.

"If successful, of course, it would force a General Election. Are we ready?"

Paxton Turnquest had been Party strategist for the past two elections, maintaining the Executive position of Deputy Chairman, a post which placed him in a position of confidence while allowing him to avoid major public exposure. Miller could not have designed a more accommodating question.

"No. But that is not the question. They are in worse shape than we are, especially if what you say is true. The economy is down, they haven't completed any projects to show, and the one project they have is a huge white elephant, causing internal party trouble. I say it's a perfect time."

"I don't know, Fred. The Election next year anyway, right? If we try this thing an' it don't work we'll be hurt'n ourse'f for the General election. I don't know."

That was Rev, the oldest member of the Executive, a former Member of Parliament under a Labor banner. He had left politics after the Labor party officially joined the Opposition, but was convinced to return to active politics by Freddie Miller, with the promise of an Executive position, and a possible return to Parliament. Although some people thought him pessimistic by nature, Freddie had respect for his caution, as well as his experience.

"Well, let's look at that. You might be right. An' the last thing we need right now is to give Chris anything. But lemme tell you where I stand. You remember when Cooper fought Ali in London back in the sixties? Ali was the master in the ring, with a long string'a knock-outs under his belt. Even Cooper knew he didn't stand much of a chance. So when, all of a sudden, he found himself with the Champ half-way down, sit'n on the ropes, he paused - he questioned himself. That split-second pause caused him his spot in history. Ali recovered, came back, and won the fight. If I have Chris on the ropes, I want to deliver the blow quick. I don't think we want to give him time to catch hisse'f."

Rev, had started nodding his head in agreement halfway through Freddie's speech. Everyone else in the room seemed relieved that Freddie had pointed the way so clearly. A minute later they were simply discussing the details, planning the strategy for convincing the rest of the General Council. The fact that the Executive were united in their proposal would be the major factor in the Council's decision. The vote was on.

But one day, while Tork was walking through the market, speaking to the market-women, he heard voices coming from inside a building. It sounded as if someone was arguing, but there were also the voices of a small crowd, and the occasional sound of applause. Tork, ignoring the words of his attendants, sneaked up to a window and looked in.

Inside was a tall, young man, perhaps in his early twenties, standing in front of a small group. Most of the members of the group were young, the same age as the young man speaking, and there were both men and women present. On the far side of the room stood an older man he thought he knew, but in his mind he could not name him. The young man was speaking again.

"We are supposed to be a free and civilized people, yet we have no laws except the laws of Tork, an old man who rules by dreams. Should not every one of us be equal? Should not my future depend upon what I make of it, not what Tork dreams for it? I demand a Book of Rights. I demand a guarantee of justice, with judgment by my peers. I demand a Council chosen by the people, not by an old soldier who chooses only those who would agree to his will."

Tork was furious. As the small audience applauded he gave the order to arrest them all for treason. When he returned to his palace he was disturbed, more than he had ever been. He called his Elders around and gave them their instructions.

"They are saying that I am an old man who rules unfairly, making you do my will. They say they want laws and a Book of Rights, as if they no longer trust us. I want you to deal with these traitors. Put them to death!"

As he stomped out of the room, leaving the Council to issue it's decree, there was no doubt what that decree would be. An hour later the news went out that there would be a hanging the next day.

That night, Tork hardly slept. Since his thirteenth birthday he had known that it was his duty - his only duty - to lead his people, and that his dreams were the Divine guidance he needed to be a good ruler. He had done everything in his power to make a nation they could be proud of. There was both peace and plenty. At sunrise, when the frantic knock came on his door, he was already up, pacing the floor.

During the night, the prison was attacked and the prisoners set free. On the walls outside the prison slogans had been painted, calling him a dictator. One of them called him Tork the Tyrant, and accused him of wanting to murder innocent citizens only because they wanted a democratic way of life. As his anger and confusion surged, his mind re-ran the scene of the small band of young people assembled in the back room. The older man somehow reminded him of the way his uncle would watch as he prepared his youthful army for the liberation of his people, more than thirty years ago. Then he remembered the face of the older man and in his fury smashed a water-jug on the stone floor. It was Calupa.

"I knew I should have killed him."

Tork issued the order for Calupa to be arrested on sight and to be treated as a dangerous criminal. His Council was reluctant to sanction his demand for emergency powers, so that he could put down dissidence without formalities, so he disbanded the Council and announced a State of Emergency. He summoned his army and moved his operations to a fortress high above the houses of the people. Finally, in the interest of maintaining peace, he ordered a curfew.
The people were confused. Tork had indeed been a good leader. He had fought their enemies, made friends with their neighbors, brought in the traders and the teachers. He had never been selfish in the use of his power. The request by the young people for a more organized way of ruling had come as a result of the fine education Tork had fought to provide, and they would have assumed he would be pleased at this development. Instead, he was behaving indeed like a tyrant.

As the weeks and months went by, Tork's army hunted down the young activists, although they were often disloyal, and in fact helped the dissidents, whose slogans were now appearing everywhere. So the King chose his twenty most trusted men, disguised them as civilians, and sent them out. Their job was two-fold. They were to collect information so that Tork could determine who his enemies were among the people, and they were to terrorize those known to oppose his dictatorship.

This plan worked well. Within a short time all of the known dissidents had been captured and no-one was speaking out against Tork. The State of Emergency was lifted and the Council of Elders restored. It was as if the sun was shining on Eluria again. The people were once again at ease. But behind the scene, the secret force continued to seek out even the slightest hint of disagreement. They removed those books in the schools which spoke of kingdoms where people chose their leaders, they searched visiting merchants for documents they could determine to be potentially disruptive. They banned public speeches unless the text had been agreed, and public entertainment was carefully screened.

The air was electric. As Freddie Miller crossed the National Square on his way to the House of Assembly, waving to his supporters, the die-hard group that expressed its support by standing outside Parliament and chanting slogans whenever there was a meeting, his stride hinted at his excitement. Only a handful of people knew what was about to happen, but they also knew that secrecy was essential to their success. Even the normally-effective double agents had not discovered the plan. As he nodded to the saluting policeman at the door, he grinned. The Officer was puzzled.

"Isn't it a beautiful day?"

"Mr. Speaker, Honorable Prime Minister and Members of the Cabinet, Members of this Honorable House. The people's business requires that the Government of the day have the confidence of the House..."

"Mr. Speaker, Point of Order. May I ask what item on the Agenda the Honorable Member is addressing?"

"Mr. Speaker, I rise on the People's business!"

"But with respect, Mr. Miller, there is an Agenda. Are you addressing Matters Arising........"

"...No Sir! I am addressing a matter of National urgency! I am requesting, Mr. Speaker, on behalf of the people of this country, that I be allowed to finish."

"It depends on the substance of your matter, Mr. Miller?"

"Mr. Speaker, with respect, Sir, I have a right to request that a matter be tabled. If there is space on the agenda, it must be allowed...and there is certainly space on this agenda!"

"Does Government have objection...?"

"You, Sir, are the Speaker of this House. You do not need Government's permission to do your job, Sir. The rules are clear."

Unnoticed in the mounting excitement, the Sergeant-at-Arms hands the Speaker a piece of paper. The sudden loss of color in his face halts the conversation dead in its tracks.

"Gentlemen, we have been asked to leave the Chamber quietly, but as quickly as possible. The business of the House is hereby suspended sine die... You will be advised when we shall continue."

The gavel landed before the word "suspended" had reached its mark.

"But Mr. Speaker, Sir..."

"Mr. Miller. I have no time to repeat myself. Shut up and get out."

A telephone call had warned of two bombs in the building, one of them a dummy. The caller described the dummy and its location. He had made it easy to find. As the Chamber emptied reluctantly into the Square, Members were hustled across the street by helmeted Policemen, to a small clearing in the crowd. Miller found himself standing next to Sir Christopher, choking on his frustration, wondering if the proverbial cat was out of the bag. Of course it was.

"The confidence of the House, eh? You're good. You're very good. It looks like I have some work to do before we get back together. See you soon, Mr. Miller."

As he watched the PM disappear through the thickening crowd, fighting back the panic of a lost opportunity, he felt himself being watched. Not far away, huddled together, were five frightened back-benchers. He could probably no longer count on their votes.

The midday news was chilling. The second bomb had detonated, destroying the Government's Committee Room and a portion of the northern facade. Fortunately, only one policeman was injured and the resultant fire was contained quickly. The meeting of the House had been re-scheduled for the Senate Chamber in two days, allowing for the surviving regalia to be relocated.

Before the news report was over, the first round of meetings began. Sir Christopher met with his Cabinet and designated speakers for an impending No-Confidence vote. Miller met with his Parliamentary colleagues to review the decision to proceed. Emmett Christie met with six other back-benchers to decide how much damage they had done to their Parliamentary careers, if the vote was canceled, now that Sir Christopher had time to prepare for it. The second round began by night-fall. Sir Christopher met with a group of party operatives to map out a damage control strategy and to send messages to the back-bench. Miller met with his Party officers to draft a list of key persons for posts in a still-possible new Government. Christie met his doctor for treatment for chest pains. The Commissioner of Police met with the Commanders of the Defense Force and the Reserves. The Superintendent of the Bomb Squad met with the press. Only Zed had no meetings to go to. He sat alone on the beach and read about the bombing of Parliament. Now he would write his list of demands. Now they would take him seriously.

"Ah, Mr. Christie. What can I do for you?"
"Um...er...I...er...we were wonderin' sir, if you still intend..."
"Who is 'we', Mr. Christie? You and Sir Chris?"

Freddie still enjoyed his cat-and-mouse games. He imagined Emmet Christie's discomfort at the other end of the telephone line. It must have taken a lot of courage to make this call, now that the spotlight had been aimed at the back-bench.

"The same seven."
"I don't think so. I think we'll wait for the General Election."

Silence.

There would be a full twenty-four hours before the House met again, before his motion could be tabled. In that time Sir Christopher would surely have confirmed his back-bench, one way or another. That is, unless he was certain there was no need for concern.

"You know, we would be happy to accommodate you, throw your hat into the ring, so to speak, next year. That is, if you're still interested."

He could almost hear Christie's confusion. The interruption had not only cost Freddie the element of surprise, it had raised the stakes for his back-bench support. He would now have to be very careful how much he trusted their support. Or their discretion.

"Unless, of course, there is some way of our knowing that your support is...what can I say?...secure? But then, I can't imagine you could give that kind of assurance, can you? So let's wait for the Election."

Once again there was a pause, while Christie composed his next sentence.

"Is this telephone...safe?"
"I don't know. Is yours?"
"Can I call you back in half hour?"
"Call me at this number."

Miller had memorized the number at the telephone booth in a nearby restaurant, where he sometimes met informants. Christie would not, of course, know where it was, and the chances of a security breakdown would be minimal. On the other hand, he had arranged for the telephone there to have certain conversations recorded, a fact known only to Solomon the owner, a friend and political supporter of Freddie Miller's. Freddie knew there would be few people in the restaurant at that time of day, and was chatting about the bombing with Sol when the telephone rang.

"It's for you."

Christie's tone had now become formal and he spoke quickly.

He requested a meeting, as early as possible to discuss the "future of the country" with Mr. Miller. Freddie chuckled, and suggested lunch at The Verandah, a private club of which he was a member. He would, of course, need to know who would be joining him, so that he could leave their names with the maitre'd. There would be seven guests.

Sir Christopher had not been idle. Although he had dispatched "messages", he had also personally telephoned every member of his back-bench. He made it clear that - as the saying goes - "membership has its privileges", meaning quite the opposite. He expected support, or they could expect his wrath. It was as simple as that. No member of his Party had ever, or would ever, vote against him and kept their seat in Parliament. This was serious business, and he was taking it seriously.

On the other hand, he would find ways of rewarding anyone assisting in the demise of this plot to overthrow the Government. He had also had a private meeting with the Governor-General, along with the Commissioner of Police, supposedly to review the implications of the bombing. The

Police felt it was an isolated incident. Sir Christopher disagreed.

"And I think we must take the cautious route, at all costs. We cannot afford to be mistaken. There are a lot of misguided people out there."

The three spent most of the morning reviewing their options. When they parted, there was a cautious smile on the Prime Minister's face, and the Commissioner of Police had a lot of work to do.

"Where to Sir?"
"The Flamingo Club. Let's have lunch."

But Calupa had not been caught. That was because he was not among the people. He had created his own little village in the wilderness after being chased out by Tork, where he had learned to read, and from where he was spreading the philosophies he had discovered during his years alone. He had escaped with only two of the young people, whom he encouraged to stay and study. He knew they would not. Instead, they planned the creation of a new group of dissidents, so secretly organized that Tork's secret army would have difficulty infiltrating it. They would also find a way to identify the members of the secret army, so that the public would shun them. For almost a year they planned. And while they planned they helped Calupa draft a Book of Rights, which they called a Constitution, and which they copied twelve times. Just after the New Year celebration, while Tork and his secret army slept, drowsy from wine and celebration, the three slipped across the border into Eluria,

*each carrying four copies of the Constitution, having left
the original at Calupa's camp.*

*While Calupa went to the marketplace, heavily disguised as
an old beggar, the two young men Etuk and Bordicara,
went into the towns to begin speaking to the people
privately. They quickly recruited other young people to
copy and discuss the Constitution, and within a month there
were a hundred copies in circulation and everyone was
whispering about democracy.*

*But soon Tork got hold of a copy. Once again he was
furious. The State of Emergency was immediately returned
and the secret army offered bounties for each dissident
captured. This time, however, there was less fear, and
nobody would even speak to anyone suspected of being
involved with the Secret Police. All they spoke about was
democracy.*

*Then one night it happened. Two prominent members of
the secret army were attacked by a group of shop-keepers,
irate about the rude interruption of their merchants'
meeting. The unrest spread like wild-fire, infecting
neighborhood after neighborhood with the sudden potency
of their mass action. By morning Tork looked out of his
window to find his whole country at his feet, demanding his
removal, demanding the setting up of a democratic
government. He flatly refused either.*

*That was when Calpua stepped forward. He begged the
crowds not to use violence but to lay a peaceful siege on
Tork's palace. In his arrogance, Tork had not planned for
any long-term loss of contact with his supply sources, and
would last only a short time without those supplies. The
crowd agreed, and as they set up camps around the*

fortified palace, they gathered in small groups to read about this new idea called a Constitution.

The older folk were aghast at the kinds of ideas put forward. They had always been led by someone chosen by Divine indication, like Tork's dream, or the fact that Thunder was born with twelve fingers and grey eyes. Now they were being encouraged to choose a leader by deciding among themselves who had the kind of qualities they wished in a leader. While this made sense, it was probably an insult to the gods. But the young people saw no such contradiction. They were certain it was the plan of the gods that they should become more responsible for themselves. The document also suggested that it was not the leader's right to dispense justice, its style depending completely upon his mood. It proposed the setting up of a trial system, with decisions made by groups of citizens. To support this, there would be laws written down, so that everyone would be judged on the same basis. This meant, in turn, that there would be no class divisions within the law, and every man would be equal.

For sixty days the people huddled around the fires and talked about the new way of life they would lead if Tork would only allow them. When the gates opened and he walked out, head bowed in defeat, there was a great cheer. Several of the young warriors tied him up and dragged him to the Main Square for execution, but Calupa stopped them.

"If you believe in the goodness of your new way of life, you must bring Tork to trial, so that his penalty would be fair, resulting from judgment by a group from among you, judged according to the laws you wish to uphold yourselves. If you kill him now, you would be no different from him."

Tork was taken to a place where he kept his prisoners and left there, in a dark, damp, silent cell. That night, the people of Eluria danced in the streets, and everyone was happy. Their Promised Land would at last be theirs. In his cell, Tork watched a small house-spider climb up the wall, his only company on this historic day.

"I don't understand it. My whole life I spent in the service of my people. Did I not lead them through the wilderness to this land? Did I not find them food and water in the desert....defend them against their enemies, inside and outside? Have I not established the very schools in which they have learned to read and write? How, then, can they cast me out, on the dictates of a document? I loved them all. And I was foolish enough to believe they loved me. But they never did. They only loved what I could do for them. Now they look to that coward Calupa, who has turned their head by promising them my power. My power. I knew I should have killed him."

Zed was upset. The Police had issued a statement saying that the bombing was the work of a mentally unstable individual, suffering from delusions of grandeur. They were anticipating an arrest, and no further problems. No further problems? They hadn't seen problems yet!

And the people of Eluria lived democratically ever after.

By nightfall, all was set. The resolution would proceed, as planned. The seven dissidents had pledged support, and actually signed the Memorandum of Understanding Miller had prepared. For them, it was all or nothing.
Freda poured coffee, then sat to join her obviously worried husband. They had been awakened by a telephone call from the Commissioner of Police. There had been three separate fires the previous night, all at Government-owned

properties. In each case, a hand-painted sign had warned that Government needed to listen to the people. Now they were not so sure it was the work of a single person.

"Is this going to stop your meeting today?"
"No, I don't think so. But it will distract people. This is serious."

Three separate fires destroying only Government buildings. There was certainly something serious going on. An hour later he walked into the Senate Building. This was not the same Freddie Miller who waved and smiled two days ago, whose confidence had infected the Chamber and lifted the mood. This was a worried man. The vote would probably go his way, if it went at all. But the morning news and the crowd in the Square would certainly disrupt the proceedings, and he could imagine the Speaker postponing the meeting, which would be disastrous. He hoped he could keep the plan on track for a few more hours.

The crowd in the Square had now heard that the Opposition was planning a vote of "No-Confidence". An hour before the Members began arriving, two groups formed at opposite corners of the National Square, each with hastily drawn-up placards in support of its champions. The Opposition supporters focused on the Government's careless spending, especially for their disastrous construction project, at the expense of the economy. Government's supporters touted the success of their social programs, and their very freedom.

At first they simply marched in circles, well separated by the central fountain, and under the watchful eyes of uniformed police officers. But as the numbers grew, they came closer together, and the insults began. By the time Freddie Miller arrived, the Police had had to call for reinforcements and dogs, and the insults had gone from Party to personal.

"Mr. Speaker, Sir. When we adjourned last, this Opposition had requested the tabling of an item on the Agenda. You, Sir, were in the midst of a ruling..."
"That is correct, Mr. Miller. And I will now complete my ruling. The item may be tabled, sir. It will be allowed under the heading "New Business" on the Agenda..."
"But Sir..."
"That is my ruling, Mr. Miller."

Freddie's eyes met Sir Christopher's. The latter's satisfied smile told him whose ruling the Speaker was really voicing. There would be no New Business this meeting, if Sir Christopher could stretch the debates. That was clearly the plan when Freddie Miller sat down, and debate began on a minor taxation issue. But after only a few minutes of debate, after only the presentation by the Government speaker, instead of the Shadow Minister of Finance responding, it was the Leader of the Opposition who spoke.

"Mr. Speaker, this is an important issue, one that I am surprised, after so long in office, the Government is only now bringing to this House. The very fact that they are only now dealing with this issue is indicative of their gross neglect both of the people and the economy. It is our belief that this Government does not have the confidence of this Parliament, and I therefore move a motion that this House has no confidence in the Government..."
"Second"

The silence lasted only a few seconds and was broken by a loud round of applause. Sir Christopher, his face tight with anger, slowly surveyed the room. On his own back-bench, he noted the satisfied smiles, although no-one on his side of the floor would dare clap. He had been caught by surprise, but not without a contingency plan.

"Mr. Speaker, as you are aware, our country has been under attack by forces unknown, as demonstrated by the recent bombing and fires. I have met with the Governor-General, and consulted with the Commissioner of Police. I had intended to discuss the matter with the Honorable Leader of the Opposition prior to an announcement. However, his motion has forced me to have to table this."

The Sergeant took the document to the Speaker who unfolded it ceremoniously, and handed it back to the Sergeant, with his unspoken instruction to read it to the House.

"Pursuant to Section 27 of the Constitution, and to the powers vested in the Office of the Governor-General, and upon the advice of the Prime Minister, I hereby declare a State of Emergency..."

No one in Parliament heard the rest of his Proclamation.

The crowd outside stood in shock as the Provost Marshall read the proclamation. The Police quickly hustled them out of the Square, while copies detailing the standard of public behavior in force, were pinned to the notice boards. Sir Christopher stood next to Freddie Miller in the Senate window.

"Just so you know, by the time this State of Emergency is lifted, most of your support will be gone."
"Yeah? Gone where?"
"Just gone, Bra, Gone."

Two pairs of eyes met. Freddie felt the hair on his neck stand up as the coldest pair of eyes he had ever seen seemed to burn a hole in his own, like a science-fiction probe searching for the secret files in his head. This was not a matter of democracy or politics, it was a matter of animal survival, and with his back against the wall, Sir Christopher would be a most dangerous animal.

"Mr. Miller, this is Harry Evans, I'm afraid we have a problem. I don't know how to say this, except that...er...I'm out."
"But you signed your name."
"You'll just have to sue me." (Click)

Within another hour and a half, he received four other such calls, the fifth was from Christie.

"Mr. Miller. Things have changed. Sylvia Innis is in hospital. The Police claim she tried to crash through a roadblock. Amos Chisholm's house burned down this evening. And I just got a call from someone who warned me that Sir Christopher intends to use this State of Emergency to eliminate everybody he even suspects would vote against him."

But the word was getting around. The State of Emergency was only Sir Christopher's way of avoiding the vote of No-Confidence. People were holding three-way telephone conversations about their options. Most were not pleasant.

"Hello? Inspector Wells? This is that mentally unstable individual you talked about on the news. You mean to tell me I cause this State 'a Emergency?"
"Sir, who are you? Can we meet?"

"You know better'n that. Just like you know the Government just duckin' the Vote of "No-Confidence". An' it ain' right. The people see through that, an' they just might put a stop to this foolishness."

"And just what does that mean?"

"You'll find out." (Click)

"Sir? Sir?"

***

When the group started along the Main roadway, there were three middle-aged men shouting Opposition slogans at the morning traffic. Then there were five, then ten, including four women. Within four blocks, there were a hundred. Soon they were from every conceivable background, male, female, old and young, all galvanized by anger. The bogus State of Emergency seemed to prove the Government was running scared, and had no intention of allowing a democratic ruling in the House. Sir Christopher and his cronies had been living well, spending the Treasury's money without questions for years, while the people struggled, and now they would have to be accountable to the people. They must not be allowed to use this sham. The people were marching to the National Square to demand the "No-Confidence" vote.

"Take the power back. We'll take the power back."

"NO CON-FID-ENCE! NO CON-FID-ENCE!"

"TAKE THE SWEETNESS, TAKE THE PAIN. MESS WITH US, WE'LL MAKE IT RAIN."

When Zed joined the group, they were half-way to the Square. The crowd was growing larger by the stride. Soon there would be thousands of angry citizens in the National Square, defying the State of Emergency, demanding justice. The man on the makeshift platform would be Zed.

The Inspector telephoned Sir Christopher in his limousine.
The Prime Minister assured him that he would handle the
crowd, and instructed his driver to take him to the Square.
Freddie Miller also got a call, and also turned his car
towards the Square. The PM got there first.

"My brothers and sisters. I understand your concern..."
"All you understand is spendin' my money..."
"Get away from here. Thief?"
"Now listen. I never stole a penny..."
"Thief! Thief!"
"We want Freddie Miller! We want Freddie Miller!."
"Hey, it was I who gave you everything you've got. What
did he ever give you?"
"Look to me like he's offerin' us the future. You's only the
past. Your day done."
"Hey, see Miller there. Bring him."
"Miller! Miller! Miller!"
"No, Hey! I'm the Prime Minister. You can't do this."
"Mil-ler, Mil-ler!"
"Look at what I've done. I brought you from nowhere..."
"An' you ain' bin taking us nowhere neither."
"Mil-ler, Mil-ler..."
"Officer! Officer! Stop this nonsense. Stop it, I say!"
"Mil-ler...Mil-ler, Mil-ler!"
"Hey! Officer! I'm your Prime Minister. I'm giving you an
order. Arrest that man. He's inciting a riot. Arrest him!"
"Mil-ler...Mil-ler!"

The debris left in the National Square seemed appropriate.
The nation was in shambles. The crowd had left the Square,
taking Freddie Miller on their shoulders down the Main
street, leaving the debris and six solitary figures. Sir
Christopher had propped himself up against a column in
front of the bombed-out Parliament Building. Zed sat on
the edge of the fountain watching him. He had once been a

great leader, taking the country through the War of Independence. He had founded almost all of the country's democratic institutions, and loved the country, as much as he loved himself. He could not understand their rejection, in favor of this idealistic, snot-nosed newcomer.

Zed crossed the space, watched closely by the bodyguards twenty yards away. He stopped near Sir Christopher, stared at him for awhile, then walked away. Suddenly he stopped, turned, and faced the older man.

"Do you know why Moses never made it into the Promise Land?"
Sir Christopher raised his eyes to meet Zed's, puzzled by the nature of the question.

 Zed answered his own question.

"Because he was a Warrior, and warriors are not meant to govern. They're not by nature democratic."

As Zed disappeared into the late-morning heat, towards the sound of public celebration, the bodyguards hustled a suddenly-old Sir Christopher into his car.

Will the Returning Officer at North Eleuthera please contact the Registrar General's office urgently for important information in connection with the up-coming General Elections.

www.ingramcontent.com/pod-product-compliance
Lightning Source LLC
Chambersburg PA
CBHW030346030726
47499CB00003B/930